Footloose

Footloose

A novel by Rudy Josephs based on the
screenplay by Dean Pitchford and
Craig Brewer

BLOOMSBURY

NEW YORK BERLIN LONDON SYDNEY

First published in the United States of America in September 2011
by Bloomsbury Books for Young Readers
www.bloomsburyteens.com

For information about permission to reproduce selections from this book, write to
Permissions, Bloomsbury BFYR, 175 Fifth Avenue, New York, New York 10010

Library of Congress Cataloging-in-Publication Data
available upon request
ISBN: 978-1-59990-705-5
LCCN: 2011929090

Book design by Regina Roff
Typeset by Westchester Book Composition
Printed in the U.S.A. by Quad/Graphics, Fairfield, Pennsylvania
2 4 6 8 10 9 7 5 3 1

There is a time for everything,
*   and a season for every activity under heaven:*
a time to be born and a time to die,
*   a time to plant and a time to uproot,*
a time to kill and a time to heal,
*   a time to tear down and a time to build,*
a time to weep and a time to laugh,
*   a time to mourn and a time to dance.*

—Ecclesiastes 3

Footloose

Prologue

The pulsating rhythm of the music filled her body right down to her pink Converse high-tops. She'd wanted to wear the strappy leather heels she got on her last trip into Atlanta, but she'd made that mistake before in this muddy pit of a hick town. No matter how good they looked on her, heels were for indoor activities, not wild keggers in the middle of nowhere.

The rubber soles on her sneakers bounced to the beat, stomping on the plywood along with a few dozen other sneakers, boots, and a smattering of already ruined heels. The bodies jumping and shifting on the makeshift dance floor kicked up mud along the edges, splattering the few people dumb enough to stand back and watch rather than join in. Beer sloshed around her half-empty plastic cup with each step. Hoots and hollers filled the air as they all sang along.

"I love this song!" she screamed over the pumping music to whoever was listening. She didn't know if anyone could even hear her. Didn't care, either. The music was all that mattered.

Whoever had set up the spontaneous homecoming party was a genius. It was miles away from her judgmental parents, the school that she'd graduate from at the end of the year, and the town she couldn't wait to leave behind. Only the trees were around to see her having a few sips of beer. To watch her make out with Bobby on the dance floor. To do all kinds of things she'd have to repent for in church on Sunday.

Early admittance into New York University brought the promise of more nights like this. The freedom to celebrate a life built from her own choices, from making her own mistakes. But none of that mattered now. All she wanted was to dance. *Footloose*, like the song said.

Beer spilled out of her cup and onto the plywood as she threw her arms around her best friend and her boyfriend. "I love you guys!"

The moves shifted from the uncoordinated free-for-all to a country line dance. Feet kicked up in coordinated choreography. She knew this one from hours spent in her bedroom learning the steps while her parents screamed for her to stop banging around and turn down the "noise."

Twist. Kick. Turn. Stomp. "Wahoo!"

"The party's moving!" somebody yelled in her ear. A warm, sweaty hand pulled her along. It was Bobby. Her Bobby.

Leaving him was the only regret she had about getting out of Bomont. She took another gulp of her beer, hoping to push that unhappy thought from her mind. Tonight wasn't about regrets. Tonight was for celebrating.

Bobby had led the team to homecoming victory only a few hours earlier. They'd skipped out of the official post-game party with the "returning" alumni, who had only come back from down the street. Hardly anyone ever left Bomont. None of the seniors wanted to hang out with their parents and neighbors when they could be out having fun instead. This was the unofficial homecoming celebration—the one their parents and teachers knew about, but pretended didn't exist. As if they just ignored what their kids were up to they'd still be little angels in their parents' eyes.

· · · · ·

She took her usual spot riding shotgun in Bobby's car while her best friend, Jenny, squeezed into the backseat with the boys. She was practically in Ronnie's lap. Jenny had been flirting with him for months. Tonight he finally flirted back.

It was way too early to head home. Her curfew had been extended because it was homecoming; her parents let it go on special occasions. She wasn't sure exactly where the group was going now, but wherever Bobby wanted to move the party was okay by her.

The song continued thumping out of Bobby's radio as he started the car. Jenny's brother worked the overnight shift at the local radio station, providing the commercial-free soundtrack for the party. None of the adults listened to the radio this late, so they wouldn't complain that the station had switched from its easy-listening format. Didn't matter that the song was older than she was; she kicked her pink sneakers up on the dashboard and let her toes sway along with the music.

The tires spit dirt behind them as Bobby pulled out of the spot between two sycamore trees. The sudden jolt spilled the rest of her beer in the process. "Party foul!" she hollered over the music.

Bobby only had two beers, and half of hers. She'd seen him pound down four times that watching a Bulldogs game. Not like she could have offered to drive. The beer and a half she drank was more than enough for a lightweight like her. She threw the plastic cup out the window, turned up the music, and screamed along with the lyrics. One more semester was all that was left before she was free.

A hand tapped her on the shoulder and she shifted in the seat. Jenny leaned forward, her hand needlessly pressed against Ronnie's body for support. Her mouth was moving, but her voice couldn't compete with the pounding music. It was too dark back there to even read her friend's lips.

"Can't hear you!" she shouted to Jenny.

The sudden extra light helped. Jenny was saying something about Bobby until her mouth froze and her eyes went wide.

She turned in time to see that the light came from the truck heading straight for them.

"BOBBY!"

She grabbed the wheel, but it was too late. Metal struck metal. Her body slammed against the passenger door. The car went spinning. The singing turned into screams. Her voice was still the loudest.

The car struck the guardrail with a bone-jarring jolt—then a snap. The metal rail wasn't enough to stop them. Her head hit the roof. She saw stars. Her body bounced around the passenger seat as more screams drowned out the music.

Her forehead smashed into the dashboard as the car came to a sudden stop.

But it was cold. So, so cold.

Bobby?

He didn't answer. Did she even say his name out loud? It was getting colder.

Where did the water come from?

They were in the lake. That's right. They'd been on Crosby Bridge. The water was rising. She had to get out.

The music still played, but the voices had stopped singing along. Stopped screaming.

The door didn't budge. The electric windows wouldn't open. She pressed her hand against the cracked window, trying to break out.

Pain shot up her wrist. Something in her was broken like the glass.

The water continued to rise.

She was getting tired. So tired. But the night was still young.

The water was so high.

The cold enveloped her body. It made the pain hurt less. It made the world around her quieter. Everything was quieter in the cold.

And the darkness.

The song was gone, but she could still feel the pulsing beat of the music in the water. Until she didn't feel anything anymore.

Chapter 1

Ren McCormack ran down the wide Boston street, the bags he carried banging against his body with each step. His books were on one shoulder, his gymnastics gear on the other, and the paper bag with his mom's prescription was still in his hand. There wasn't time to put it away as he dashed out of the drugstore to catch the bus. The next one wouldn't come for another half hour, and he was in no mood to wait. He hated to keep his mom waiting for him.

Mom had the car today. She needed it more than he did. All he would have used it for was to drive to and from school, leaving it parked in the lot all day while he was in class. Ren was the only freshman in his high school with a driver's license. His friends were all jealous, but he'd trade his right to drive in a heartbeat if his mom would only get better.

The bus pulled up to the stop as he got there. *Made it!* With a relieved sigh, he boarded after the other passengers, flashed his pass, and was lucky to find a lone empty seat near the middle. It was his first chance to sit since geography class.

Joining the gymnastics team was his mom's idea. She insisted on it, really. Kept pushing him to be a normal teen. Like he had any idea what normal was. But he had always liked gymnastics when he was younger.

His dad had signed him up for basketball at the local Y when he was in grade school, back when Dad was still around. Basketball lasted about a week. Ren wasn't big on organized team sports like that, even as a kid. He preferred teams that let him do his own thing. The gymnastics class met at the same time in the gym beside the basketball court. It was mostly girls, but Ren didn't care. He switched over to that class on his own. His dad hadn't even noticed.

An older woman got on the bus a few stops later and Ren gave up his seat to her. She almost refused when she saw all the stuff he carried, but Ren wouldn't let her. It wasn't right for him to sit there while she had to stand. Of course, the kids in the seats two rows back acted like they didn't notice any of it.

It was only a few more blocks home, anyway. He could have walked, but he was too tired from practice. Mom was right. It was fun. He'd already made some friends he probably never would have spoken to in school other-wise. Coach even talked about a trip abroad next year, but Ren knew he'd never go. He couldn't leave his mom for that long.

Ren maneuvered his bags so that he could take his iPod out of the backpack and queue up his favorite play-list. Music always relaxed him. Between school and doc-tors and now gymnastics, his mind was always running. But when he had the earbuds in and the music cranked up, he could zone out for a while and let it all go.

Before he knew it, the bus was at his stop. He almost missed it, actually. If it hadn't been for the group of kids shoving past him on their way out he would have day-dreamed his way to the next stop, or maybe farther. He'd done that a few times before and had to walk back home. Usually it happened when a good song came up on shuffle.

Ren hopped off the bus and hurried up the stairs to his apartment. "Mom?" he called out.

No answer.

That was odd. Even on the days she ran errands after her part-time job in the morning, she was usually home when he got there. Stranger still, there was no note on the fridge telling him where she was. He made a quick search of the apartment to make sure everything was okay. It didn't take long—it was only a one-bedroom. Ren slept on the pullout couch in the living room. They called it the "Master Suite" to make it seem like he got the better end of the deal, since his room was twice the size of his mom's.

She wasn't in the "Guest Room" or the bathroom, either. Probably just running late on one of her errands, but Ren couldn't help feeling a nagging worry. He felt that way a lot, usually for no reason. Mom always made fun of him for it. Called him a worrywart. But he knew she hated that he worried about her so much.

While on his search of the place, he noticed that the bathroom hadn't had a good cleaning in a while. He needed to get on that. It wasn't good when things got all germy around the apartment. There were health issues to consider.

He pulled his headphones out of the iPod and attached the small portable speakers so he could fill the apartment with music. Mom liked coming home to music. Not just stuff from her generation—she'd listen to Ren's favorite bands as well. They always had music playing when they were home. He even made her a special playlist to relax her while she was on dialysis.

Ren was elbow-deep in the toilet bowl, singing along to the music, when the front door burst open.

"Ren? Ren!"

"In the bathroom!"

"Well, get out here, I've got news!"

"Be right there."

Ren went to the sink to wash his hands. He barely had them soaped up when his mom called for him again.

"I'm coming!" he shouted back. He didn't know why she kept calling him. The door was open—she could just walk down the hall.

He dried his hands and went out to the living room. His mom was dancing to the song on the iPod when he came out. When she saw him, she struck a pose like she was showing off a new outfit, but everything she was wearing was the same as when he'd left for school. Not even her hair had changed. "Guess what?" she asked.

"What?"

"The doctor said my condition is stabilizing. I might even be able to stop dialysis soon!"

The music still played, but Ren couldn't hear anything but the pounding of his own heartbeat. Did Mom say what he thought she said? Was there finally a light at the end of this long, dark tunnel? Some hope that she could really get better? He could scarcely believe it. "Seriously?" he asked.

She smiled. "You're not getting rid of me yet."

Ren ran up and hugged his mom with the most delicate squeeze his excitement would allow. Once she was stronger he'd be able to hug her with all his might, but until then he had to be careful with her.

When they broke free, his mom started moving to

the beat. "This calls for a celebration," she said. "Turn up the music."

Ren did as she said, then took his mom's hand and they danced.

· · · · ·

Ariel Moore grasped her mother's hand as the tears flowed down her face. It had been a couple weeks since Bobby's death. Her big brother was already in the ground. In the dark, cold ground. Alone.

The pile of flowers and candles left in tribute outside the chain-link fence surrounding Bomont High School had been refreshed a few times. The collection of photos and cards somehow kept growing, as if every memento in the town was on display.

Bobby and his friends were gone. Ariel even missed his girlfriend, whom she never really liked. It didn't stop Ariel from blaming the girl, though. She'd been so pushy about leaving the official homecoming party at school. Sure, the party was lame, but Ariel was there. Bobby wouldn't have left her if his girlfriend hadn't made him.

These were the horrible thoughts filling Ariel's head. She shouldn't have them. Not now, not ever again. Her father would be so disappointed.

None of the seniors stayed for the party—it was mainly just freshmen and their parents. But everyone in town blamed Bobby for the accident, because he was the driver. It was only fair that someone else share the guilt, at least as far as Ariel was concerned.

"He is testing us," Ariel's daddy said to everyone gathered. The reverend was preaching to his congregation, but they weren't in church. It was an official city council meeting, one where nobody would protest the mix of church and state if the councilman/reverend/ grieving father wanted to say a few words.

"Our Lord is testing us," Reverend Shaw Moore continued. "Especially now, when despair consumes us. When we ask our God, 'Why? Why has this happened?'"

That was just one of the questions Ariel wanted answered. The other big one was, Why were all these people around her so angry? Why did they have to blame Bobby? It was an accident. A horrible accident. What was the point of blaming *anyone*?

"No parent should ever know the horror of burying their own child," Daddy said from his council seat. "And yet, five of Bomont's brightest have lost their lives. When it comes to Bomont's most precious export, we're not talking about cotton or corn. Our most precious export is our children."

Ariel's momma squeezed her hand tighter as her daddy's eyes locked onto her. Both her parents hovered around her more since the night of Bobby's death. That horrible night. Nobody even thought to wake her. They wanted her to sleep—like a child. Like a baby too young to hear the news. She got up the next morning and had to ask why everyone was in the house. Why they were crying. Why Daddy was off on town business already.

Her parents had been watching her ever since, their eyes never going too far from her . . . making sure she didn't leave the house. That they always knew where she was. It was nice to have them near, but suffocating at the same time.

"One day they will no longer be in our embrace, or in our care," Daddy continued. She could sense that he wanted to get out of his chair. He usually gave his sermons standing behind his lectern, not sitting in his council seat. "They will belong to the world—a world filled with evils and temptation and danger. But until that day, they are ours to protect." Momma held on even tighter. "*This* is the lesson to take from this tragedy. This is our test. We cannot be missing from our children's lives."

Ariel didn't get that last part. Her parents weren't missing. If anything, they were too smothering. It made sense, considering, but it was also hard on her. Sometimes she just wanted to be alone. To grieve on her own. In her own way.

Principal Dunbar took over the proceedings. He was holding together better than Ariel's father, but that wasn't a surprise. He never got emotional when there were students around. He suffered a loss, too, but she never expected him to show it in public.

"The following measures will be read and voted on accordingly," Principal Dunbar read from the sheet in

14

front of him. Ariel had seen a copy of that paper on the desk in her daddy's study, so she knew what was about to happen. Everyone had heard the talk, but she was one of the few that knew for certain.

"A curfew for minors under the age of eighteen will take effect immediately," Principal Dunbar said. "Minors will be expected to be home by ten p.m. on weeknights and eleven p.m. on the weekends. All in favor, say 'aye.'"

The council responded quickly with their unanimous "Ayes." Principal Dunbar slammed the gavel onto the desk to mark the vote. Ariel didn't much mind the curfew; that was already the rule for her, anyway. It was Bobby's curfew when he was her age, but her parents would let it slide occasionally. Now that it was a law, that flexibility was gone.

Principal Dunbar continued to read from the list of new rules. "Punitive measures will be taken against any individual, group, or property owner who organizes a public gathering where minors engage in inappropriate activities." The gavel smacked down on the desk again. "Such activities include the consumption of alcohol or unlawful drugs, inappropriate sexual activity, listening to vulgar or demeaning amplified music, or participating in lewd or lascivious dancing. All in favor, say 'aye.'"

"Aye," the council echoed.

This rule made less sense to Ariel, even after she'd seen it for herself and had time to think about it. "Inappropriate" was such a vague word. Who was going to determine what was inappropriate? She got the part about drinking and drugs. But what made dancing "lewd"? Her parents grew up in the seventies. There was a lot of lewd dancing going on back then, even in Bomont.

Ariel flinched with the bang of the gavel, as if the *crack* of the wood was the sound of her freedom disappearing.

"A dress code will take effect at the beginning of the next school year," the principal said, with an even faster drop of the gavel. This one was the easiest rule to make, she'd heard Daddy say. It was also the one that in no way would have stopped what happened to Bobby. She had wanted to point that out, but she held her tongue. This wasn't the time to argue.

They were coming up on the last new law. It was the one her friend, Rusty, had been asking her about since the funeral. She couldn't believe it was true. But Ariel knew it was. She'd seen it in black and white.

"There will be no public displays of dancing unless supervised as part of a school, civic, or church-related function," the principal read. There was surprisingly little reaction to this announcement from anyone. All she heard were the muffled sobs that had been running throughout the meeting. "Outside of these authorized institutions, public dancing among Bomont's minors will be in violation of the law. All in favor, say 'aye.'"

The council was a little slower to vote on this one. Ariel could understand why. It wasn't like Bomont had a hopping club scene, but it meant no more dancing at barbecues or parties or any random event. It meant no more fun just for the sake of having fun.

One by one, the council members announced their support of the law. Ariel should have said something when she saw the list on her daddy's desk—at least asked him about it, but that was not the time. It was clear enough that her daddy knew she didn't like the laws. She could see it when their eyes locked as the vote came to him.

"Reverend?" Principal Dunbar said. "Your vote, please."

Don't do it, Daddy.

With his eyes still on his daughter, Reverend Moore cast the last "aye" vote, making it a law.

Chapter 2
Three Years Later

The uneven rhythm of the wheels of the Greyhound bus lulled Ren into a stupor. Random thumps and thuds made up the soundtrack of his ride as they rolled over potholes and more roadkill than he'd ever seen on the streets of Boston. He wished he could listen to his iPod, but the battery completely drained four states back. This was the third bus he'd been trapped on in over thirty hours with not nearly enough rest stops. His back hurt, his neck ached, and both his feet were asleep, but he still couldn't get excited that he was close to getting off the bus for good. He wasn't looking forward to reaching his final destination.

The sign outside the oversize bus window told him he was almost there: Bomont, Georgia. Population: 11,780. It was smaller than the student body of Boston College. That's where Ren wanted to go when he dared to dream about college. Mainly because he wanted to stay close to home. But "home" didn't really mean what it used to.

The bus rumbled into a town square lined by old brick buildings. The square was fairly busy for an early Saturday. Some kind of farmers' market was set up, with people selling fruits and vegetables they probably picked off their land that morning. *How quaint.*

They had something like that in his old neighborhood in Boston, too, for a couple hours every third Saturday of the month. Ren always found nice deals there, and would stock up on dinner for the week when it was his turn to do the shopping. The food was good, but he really went back for the crazy mix of characters.

In his old neighborhood, wanna-be Rastafarians haggled with upwardly mobile urban professionals over the price of strawberries. Street performers painted their bodies in silver and gold, playing bongos one week and violins the next. The drag queen still working her way home from a Friday night of club-hopping was a regular.

The local color in Bomont was a bit blander. Jeans and T-shirts were the norm. Every now and then, khakis and polos mixed in. It was a small town lost in time. Even the freshly scrubbed kids licking their ice cream cones were straight out of one of those old Norman Rockwell paintings that seemed to be in every doctor's office he'd ever walked into.

Ren wasn't a Norman Rockwell type. He preferred Jackson Pollock or Picasso. Those were the paintings he ran to when his mom took him to the museum on the free Wednesday nights when he was a kid. A lifetime ago.

The bus pulled up to the curb with a squeal and a hiss that echoed Ren's feelings about the place. He grabbed his bag from the overhead rack and made his way down the aisle. The sum total of his worldly possessions had fit in the old army-style duffel he used to use for his gymnastics equipment. Everything else, including the car, had been sold to pay the medical bills and funeral expenses.

The bus door quickly shut behind him and the driver pulled out, leaving him alone on the curb. Nobody else got off at the stop. He was the only person whose destination was Bomont.

With a sigh of fresh country air, Ren started off on the route he barely remembered from his last visit. The place seemed bigger back then, but only because he'd been much smaller. That was back before his mom got sick . . . back when their only problem was a disappearing dad, which wasn't that big a problem at all.

Ren waited for a slow-moving train to pass, then crossed the tracks, heading for Warnicker Auto Sales. His uncle's dealership didn't look a bit different than it had on his last visit years earlier. The only thing that changed were the cars. A few of them might even have been around back then, too.

It was impossible to believe that the girls sitting in the front seat of a convertible up on a display lift were his cousins. Sarah looked nothing like the little toddler he remembered from his last trip to Bomont. Amy hadn't even been born yet. According to the last birthday cards his mom had made him sign for them, Sarah was nine now, Amy six.

The girls were having a blast in the car. Probably imagining it was taking them the hell out of Bomont.

Sarah was behind the wheel, pretending to drive, while Amy was in the seat next to her. At first, Ren thought she was waving to him, but he quickly realized she was greeting the imaginary friends they passed on their imaginary ride. That changed when her head swiveled in Ren's direction and the waving got more frantic. "Momma!" Amy called. "It's Ren! He's here!"

Nothing like the wild excitement of a six-year-old to make a person feel welcome. Both girls climbed out of the car and ran toward Ren, screaming his name, while Uncle Wesley and Aunt Lulu finished up with a customer. Ren dropped his bag as the girls jumped into his arms, wrapping him in the kind of exuberant hugs he hadn't felt in a while.

"I wanted you to sleep in my room, but Mom said you couldn't," Amy said with the disappointment of child who doesn't realize there's a difference between being six and seventeen.

"Jump back," Ren said, playing along. "I thought you and me were going to build a fort."

Sarah was a little more reserved than her sister, but still beamed happily at Ren. "What's up, Sarah?" he asked as they both clung to him. "Jeez, you girls are huge."

He managed to break free as Aunt Lulu reached them. Her hug was less excited, but still full of emotion, as if she was passing along a silent message of support with her embrace. "Hey, darlin', I hope you got some sleep on that bus."

"I got enough," Ren said as they let go of one another. "No worries, Lulu."

Ren expected to see his mother's reflection in his uncle's face, but it was still like a punch to the gut to have eyes like hers full of life again. They weren't identical by any means, but close enough that Ren felt a pang of loss. "Hey, Wesley," he said, extending his hand.

"Wesley?" his uncle asked as they shook. "Used to call me 'Unky Wes.' You too big in the britches for that?"

Ren just smiled, not sure if his uncle was joking. He'd been calling adults by their first name for years. Nurses. Insurance providers. Bill collectors. It helped put him on equal footing with people much older than him.

"He's not a baby anymore," Lulu said. "He's a grown-ass man."

Sarah giggled. "Momma said 'ass.'"

"Sarah, mind your language," Wes said.

"Lord have mercy," Lulu said lightly. "Anybody hungry?"

Ren wasn't just hungry, he was starving. His last

meal was runny eggs and burnt toast at some diner over the state line at the crack of dawn. Ren could usually eat anything in front of him, but that food was particularly foul. He'd left most of it swimming in grease on the plate.

Wes left the dealership in the hands of one of his salesmen and they piled into the family car. Ren wanted to do some sightseeing so he could get his bearings as they went through town, but Amy and Sarah hit him with so many rapid-fire questions about Boston, they took all his attention.

Wes and Lulu probably warned them about asking him any questions about his mom, because the girls steered clear of that subject. That was fine with Ren. He wasn't ready to talk about her final months, after things had taken a turn for the worse earlier that year. He wasn't sure how much the girls knew about all that, but he doubted they had heard much. They probably just knew that the aunt they'd only met a few times was sick, and that the cousin to whom they spoke on the phone every few weeks was now coming to live with them.

Like the car lot, Wes's house was exactly as Ren remembered it. Not much in Bomont seemed to change, as far as Ren could tell. He already worried that he was going to get frozen in time like the town and never get out. His mom wouldn't like him thinking that way—not even inside his uncle's house yet, and he was already dreaming of escape.

The girls ran inside so they could change into their bathing suits. They'd told Ren all about their little wading pool on the way home.

The air was hot and humid enough that he almost took them up on their offer to join them in the cool water, but Ren didn't have a bathing suit. He barely had any shorts. A recent growth spurt shot him out of most his wardrobe, and there wasn't a lot of cash on hand to replace everything. He was happy to play the part of the big cousin, holding out the hose to spray the girls and enjoying the cool mist of water while his aunt and uncle cooked on the grill.

It only took a few minutes for lunch to be ready. The girls dried off, and everyone gathered around the picnic table in the backyard. Ren took an empty spot between Amy and Sarah to avoid the argument that was brewing about who got to sit next to him.

Lunch smelled delicious. Something about a cookout made the burgers and hot dogs in front of him seem more special. They never cooked out much back home.

He was about to dig in when Amy's little hand tugged on his. Ren stopped himself in time to see everyone else around the table take hands to form a circle. He quickly pulled his arm back from the food and placed his left hand in Amy's and his right in Sarah's.

"Okay," Wes said. "Whose turn is it?"

Sarah looked up at her cousin. "I was next, but now Ren is sitting at the table. Shouldn't it be his turn?"

"My turn for what?" Ren asked. He suspected that he knew the answer, but was hoping he was wrong.

"Saying grace," Amy said simply.

Damn. He wasn't wrong. Ren didn't have much of a relationship with God. Over the years, he'd cursed Him almost as much as he'd prayed to Him. Even then, his prayers were more straightforward requests, like "Don't let my mom die." He didn't know any real prayers.

"Yeah," he said, stalling. "I don't know that I'd be too good at that. Why don't you just skip me and have Sarah do it?"

Thankfully, his uncle didn't press the issue. Wes simply nodded to his eldest daughter. "Go on, sweetheart. Knock it outta the park."

"Okay," Sarah said. "Everybody bow their heads."

Ren watched as Wes, Lulu, and the girls closed their eyes and lowered their heads. He thought about doing the same, but it would just be for show. He didn't have much to say to God. Nothing nice, anyway. He just sat there, staring off into space, wondering what he was doing in Bomont and how he was going to get out.

Chapter 3

So this was it. The place Ren would call home until he graduated. His new bedroom wasn't much more than a ten-by-ten box with a bed, dresser, and a tiny bathroom off to the side, but for someone used to less, it was more than enough.

This was the first time in years that he had his own room with a door he could shut when he wanted to be alone. Even better, it was his own personal space, built off the garage and totally separate from the house. The room had its own entrance and didn't share walls with anyone except the garage attached to it. Less chance of his aunt or uncle telling him to turn his music down.

Ren got the impression that he was taking over his uncle's personal space. The window looking out into the mess of the garage suggested that the room wasn't originally designed for guests. He couldn't remember even being in this room on his other visits.

"Used to be my office," Wes confirmed as they scoped out the room. "But Lulu fixed her up for you. Got all the essentials: water, power." Ren caught something of a wistful tone in his uncle's voice, like he just lost his man cave—the one place he could get away from all the females in the family.

"Look," Ren said. "I know you're not over the moon about this, taking me in and all. But I appreciate what you're doing here."

"Just remember, this ain't Boston," Wes said. "You give people attitude, you'll get it right back. So start sayin' your 'Yessirs' and 'No'ms.' "

"What's 'No'm'?" Ren asked. "Like those little guys with the pointy hats?"

"No, that's a garden gnome," Wes replied. " 'No'm' is 'no, ma'am.' Just lazier." His uncle sighed. "Look, just give people respect and you'll get it back. Understand?"

Of course he understood. It wasn't like Ren was running wild up in Boston, like he didn't have any manners. Being a jerk didn't help when the electric company was threatening to cut the power.

"I want to pull my own weight around here," Ren said. "That means cooking meals. Getting work."

"Well, that's good, 'cuz I already got you a job," Wes said, looking quite proud of himself.

Ren couldn't imagine many jobs in Bomont that he'd be right for. "You did?"

Wes grinned with pride. "My buddy, Andy Beamis, runs a cotton mill up on Chulahoma. He told me you could start the middle of next week."

Cotton mill? Ren didn't even know they existed anymore. The only time he'd ever heard about cotton mills was in his history books. He had no idea what to say, so he was just silent.

"You're welcome," Wes added.

Ren knew he should show some appreciation, but he couldn't imagine what he was even expected to do at that kind of job. "Couldn't I work at the car lot with you?" he asked. "I'm good with engines and oil changes. That's how I made cash back home." He was also a delivery boy, stocked shelves at the grocery store, and did some telemarketing. None of those jobs prepared him for work at a cotton mill.

"In this economy, that's the best I got," Wes said. "I suggest you learn to love it."

Wes moved through the doorway that led into the garage without waiting for a response. Ren figured he was supposed to follow, so he did.

The garage was in even worse shape than it looked through the window. It was a mess of random oil-covered car parts and tools. There was even a big loudspeaker contraption that Ren was pretty sure was some kind of tornado siren. The stacks of junk surrounded the tarp-covered body of some large, lumpy thing in the center of the room. He didn't want to see what was under the sheet.

Ren carefully stepped between the debris. "So, how am I supposed to get to work and school?" he asked. "You got subways out here in Mayberry?"

"There's that Yankee sarcasm I been hearing about. Wish it were funnier," Wes said. "Okay, you say you're good with engines? I'll make you a deal. You get this baby running, she's all yours."

Wes pulled the smelly tarp off the lump to reveal the oldest, poorest excuse for a beat-up vehicle Ren had ever seen. It was an ancient faded-yellow Volkswagen Beetle. The front was propped up on a cinder block because one of the tires was missing. So was the metal trunk cover. The rear engine sat out, exposed to the world.

The car probably hadn't even been outside of the garage since before Ren was born. "This?" he asked. "You're serious?"

Sarah bounced into the garage. "Daddy, Momma says T-minus two minutes till kick off."

"Shit," Wes said, already choking on the word as it came out of his mouth in front of his daughter. "I mean, shoot. *Heck*. Sarah, go tell Momma I'm on the way."

Ren's little cousin scurried off back to the house. Neither of the girls seemed to walk anywhere if they could skip instead.

When Ren turned back, he caught his uncle staring

at him intensely. Wes must have realized what he was doing, because he snapped out of it. "I swear, you look just like your dad."

It wasn't a compliment. "Yeah? Well, I'm not crazy about it, either."

Wes went off to his television, leaving Ren alone in the wreckage of the garage with the car that was now his, if he could get it to move under its own power. That was going to be a challenge, but it wasn't like there was all that much else to do in this small town. His only other option was to watch two football teams he didn't care about play a game that meant nothing to him.

He grabbed a toolbox off the shelf, revealing a Quiet Riot poster on the garage wall. Maybe there was a side of Uncle Wes that wasn't so uptight. The fact that the poster was hidden in the garage confirmed Ren's suspicion about the whole "man cave" thing. It also inspired him to pull out his iPod, which he'd recharged during lunch.

Quiet Riot pounded through his earbuds as Ren leaned into the open trunk to get to the engine. It looked nothing like the engines he was used to working on, but the basic parts were still the same. It didn't seem as bad on the inside as on the outside, but there was still some work to do.

Out of the corner of his eye, Ren caught Sarah and Amy watching him. They were in the yard, looking through a small, dusty window. He could tell they were talking about him. No surprise. He was a new mystery in their lives, the cousin they barely knew. He liked the idea of being sort of a big brother. It was only him and his mom up in Boston. Being part of a family was something new; equal parts comforting and terrifying.

The air quickly grew oppressive as he worked inside the small garage. Ren looked forward to a milder winter than he was used to up north, but he wasn't sure if the trade-off in heat and humidity was worth it. He wiped the sweat from his brow, rolled his iPod into his shirtsleeve to keep it safe, and got down to the nitty-gritty.

There was an old tire leaning up against the wall that was the same size as the one missing from the car. That was lucky. The engine work was also less involved than he feared it would be. The main problem turned out to be something similar to a problem he'd had with his old car a year ago. All it took was a few twists of the wrench, getting rid of a useless part, and jury-rigging the car in a way that was probably illegal, but he figured he could at least get it started.

Ren sat behind the wheel and silently promised the car some high-octane premium gas if the engine turned over when he keyed the ignition. A few chokes, a cough, and a gasp later, the vehicle slowly came to life. He revved the engine to give it a jolt, and pronounced it alive and ready for a test drive. The work was far from done, but it was good enough to get him around town until he could afford a major overhaul.

The ancient radio let out a burst of static when Ren turned it on. He adjusted the old-fashioned knob in search of stations, but heard nothing but more static and sports radio, which was the equivalent of static in his mind. That wasn't going to work. He would never survive in this town without his music.

Ren bit off his iPod's earbuds, exposing the tiny copper wires in his headphone cables. A quick twist attached them to the wires of the car's speakers, and Quiet Riot pumped out around him. Better, but not quite good enough.

His eyes focused on the derelict tornado siren lying abandoned in the corner.

Perfect.

There was one shot in a million that the dusty old thing still worked, but it was worth a try. Ren yanked it off the pile of junk and slipped it under the empty hood. A few more tweaks to the system and he'd be in business.

The Riot wasn't so Quiet anymore as the music shook the garage, causing his cousins outside to cover their ears. The car gave a jolt and a shimmy as he pulled it out of the garage and past the girls, now dancing in the driveway. The song wasn't really in their teeny-bopper repertoire, but they didn't care. They were having a blast.

Ren circled them twice in the backyard before pulling out into the street, heading off to explore.

When he saw Wes in the rearview mirror, he shouted, "Bean Town!" Score one for the city boy.

This minor triumph improved Ren's entire day. Sure, he was stuck in the middle of nowhere and knew almost no one. But he had wheels. And he had music. That was enough for now.

Time to explore.

The old country road was like something out of a retro-picture postcard, with its abandoned junkyard and an old barn with a classic Coca-Cola sign. There was even a water tower with BOMONT painted in tall letters on its side.

He pulled into the parking lot of a do-it-yourself car wash to make a U-turn, attracting a lot of attention from the locals. Some of them were kids his age. He'd probably see them again when he started school on Monday. There were a couple girls he definitely wouldn't mind meeting. He considered stopping to say hi, but changed his mind and just waved to them as he pulled back onto the road.

He'd already driven the entire length of the town. It was time to explore beyond the borders of Bomont.

Ren aimed the Bug down the two-lane blacktop and pushed the car to its limits, quickly finding that he could barely make the speed limit. Just knowing the car gave him access to the rest of the world was enough for now; it didn't matter that it would take some time to get there.

He pulled up alongside a slow-moving train, matching it for speed and volume. He sang along with Quiet Riot, drowning out the engine of the train. He swore he heard the engineer blow the horn in echoing response.

The flashing red and blue lights in the rearview mirror killed the mood. The speedometer showed that he was right on the speed limit, so it couldn't be that. Maybe he had a taillight out or something.

Ren drifted to the side of the road, cut the engine and the music, and used the manual crank to roll down the window. An officer who looked about his uncle's age, or maybe a little younger, was already beside him by the time the struggling window made it all the way down.

"Step out of your vehicle, son," the officer said in a no-nonsense tone.

Ren did as he was told. "Is there a problem, officer?"

"Driver's license?" the officer said in response. His nametag read HERB. Ren wasn't sure if that was a first name or a last, but he handed his license over to Officer Herb without comment.

"Massachusetts, huh?" the officer asked. "You got that music cranked pretty loud, Mr. McCormack."

"You going to throw me in jail for playing Quiet Riot?" Ren meant it as a joke, but it fell flat.

Officer Herb flicked Ren's chin with his license. "Let's watch that attitude."

"Yankee sarcasm," Ren mumbled.

"What's that?"

"Nothing," Ren said. He remembered his uncle's warning and quickly added, "Sir."

"You'll have to appear in court." The officer was already writing out a ticket. Ren still wasn't sure why he'd been pulled over.

"For what?" Ren was genuinely confused.

"Disturbing the peace." Officer Herb motioned toward the deserted countryside. "Isn't this peaceful?"

Ren bit back more of his Yankee sarcasm.

Officer Herb ripped the ticket off his pad and handed it to Ren. "Welcome to Bomont."

Chapter 4

The car horn blew for the third time as Ariel raced out the front door. She threw her bag into the backseat of Rusty's Mustang hatchback and hopped in the passenger seat. "Sorry. My nails wouldn't dry and they got smudged and I had to do 'em all over again."

"As long as it was something important that kept me waiting," Rusty said with an annoyed sigh as she pulled out into the street. "It's only your daddy's church. Why should we ever be on time?"

It was going to be one of *those* days. Ariel used to think that Rusty just needed a bigger caffeine fix in the morning. But it wasn't like that at all. On school or church days, the later Ariel was, the more sarcastic Rusty got. But it wasn't like Ariel didn't have a good reason to be late. She held out her fingernails for Rusty to see. "Tell me this wasn't worth the wait."

Rusty eyed the bright red nail polish. "It doesn't go with your dress."

"Nothing does." Ariel had on a flowery beige dress and the itchy green sweater her grandmomma bought her two Easters ago. She hated the outfit, but she wasn't about to waste her money on church clothes when she could spend it on more fun things—like a bottle of pricey nail polish that was a perfect match for her *other* clothes.

"What's the sermon for today?" Rusty asked. "'Protecting the Children,' 'Sin and Struggles,' or 'The Dangers of Progress'?"

"Aren't they all the same?" Ariel asked. "Bet you he finds a way to work all three in."

Rusty turned onto Main Street. "Uh-uh. I ain't falling for that one again. No betting. I haven't been able to look at Pixy Stix since grade school."

Ariel laughed. She and Rusty used to bet Pixy Stix over what the Sunday sermon would be. Ariel had a pretty good winning streak going until Rusty figured out that she used to sneak into her daddy's study to see what he was working on every week. Ariel had to give Rusty a year's worth of candy to make up for cheating her.

Betting wasn't as much fun these days, since Daddy kept cycling through the same old lessons over and over again. It had been like that for the past three years.

Ariel's family didn't live far from the church, so the ride was short. Considering how far away they had to park, they might as well have just walked. Daddy's services always played to a packed house. Not because they were exciting; he was just the biggest act in town.

This one was no different from the others Ariel had sat through on many other Sundays. When she was younger, she listened with rapt attention, believing her daddy held the answers to the mysteries of the universe. Now she understood that he was simply giving his opinion on how the people of Bomont should live their lives. Funny how much less she agreed with him these days.

Today's topic was "Progress: What Does It Mean to You?"

The reverend looked out over his congregation. "As a society, we welcome invention. We welcome ideas and industry." Ariel could already hear it coming. "*But*—there is cause for concern. There is a 'progress trap,' in which we step forward and fall behind, all at the same time."

He went on to tell the story of old Mr. Rucker, a man who had died before Ariel was even born. She'd heard a lot about him over the years. It was Daddy's favorite way of expounding on what had gone wrong with the world. She could tell the tale by heart now.

Old Mr. Rucker used to be a teller at the bank, way back before ATMs popped up in Bomont. He gave out a piece of Bazooka chewing gum when anyone made a deposit. It always made Daddy feel special. Ariel figured Old Man Rucker had some special deal with the local dentist to give all the customers cavities and increase business. But she was cynical like that.

Rusty elbowed Ariel in the side. She was always nudging her, pointing out new things. Rusty had this excited way of seeing the world that was exhausting after a while. There wasn't much in Bomont worth getting excited over.

The thing that grabbed Rusty's attention today was actually something worth noticing: a new boy sat across the aisle with the Warnicker family. One of the little girls was using his arm as a pillow. It was actually kind of adorable.

Rusty wasn't exactly subtle when she noticed something, so it was no surprise when he turned to look at them. Now that Ariel saw more than just his profile, she had to admit he was pretty cute. A shame she had to see him for the first time in church. This was not the kind of outfit she liked to wear when making a first impression.

Ariel shrugged dismissively for both Rusty's benefit and the boy's. Didn't do her any good for guys to think she was interested. It gave them too much power. When she played hard to get, it wasn't a game. It was real.

Ariel turned her attention back to her daddy at the pulpit. It sounded like he'd be wrapping up soon, if he stuck to the script.

"Why take a family vacation when you can watch TV together on the couch?" he asked rhetorically. She suspected that she inspired that line. It sounded a lot like what she said to him when he suggested a trip to the Grand Canyon. She meant it seriously at the time, but he used it sarcastically here. Ariel wasn't opposed to a family vacation, but her dream destinations were a bit more tropical.

This brought him to the part about the evils of television, especially reality television. Ariel didn't disagree that there was a lot of junk on TV, but reality shows were such easy targets. "*This* is our social network." He held his hands out over the congregation, building to a crescendo. "And we don't need Facebook to do it." He picked up the Bible. "There's only one book we need."

The laughter and smattering of applause didn't surprise Ariel. The congregants always let Reverend Shaw Moore know when they approved of his message. Ariel gave him points for the use of props with the closing bit. She subtracted points for everything else. But she had other kinds of social networking on her mind. Her eyes were glued to the new text message on her phone.

YOU COMING TONIGHT?

About time. She'd been waiting all morning for Chuck to call or text. Obviously she was going to meet up with him later, but a girl liked to be asked. She didn't just go places uninvited.

Daddy added a final endnote to his anti-innovation message. "I know that my Redeemer lives. He lives in all of us. And through His love we will be delivered to the

Kingdom of Heaven. And that . . . is the only kind of progress we need."

Ariel quickly typed,

HELL YEAH!

"Let us pray."

* * * * *

It took all Ren's willpower to keep from springing out of the pew the moment the service ended. He couldn't remember the last time he'd been in an actual church. His mom's funeral was just a small memorial service at the funeral home. Aside from Ren, the only people who'd attended were a few of the nurses they'd become friends with over the years. Uncle Wes had asked the reverend to say a few words here during his regular Sunday service; otherwise his mom's burial went largely unnoticed in the world. To everyone but Ren, that is.

It took some time for them to get up the aisle and out of the church. The delay gave Ren more time to check out the girl who had been eyeing him during the service. Sure, she'd shrugged him off, but he'd been on the receiving end of a lot of casual indifference over the years. It didn't mean that door was closed to him.

Once they were back outside the redbrick church, Ren started to head for the car, but his uncle guided the family in the other direction. The reverend and his wife were greeting the parishioners as they left the building.

"Reverend Moore," Wes said, making sure that Ren was beside him. "This is my sister's son. The one I was telling you about: Ren McCormack."

The reverend's handshake was stiff and formal. "Hey, Ren. I'm glad you're here with us today. This is my wife, Violet."

Her grip was more relaxed as she shook hands with Ren. "Hello, Ren. You can call me Vi. Everyone does." She took a shallow breath and looked him in the eye. He knew what was coming next. It had already happened a few times before the service started. "You know, I went to grade school with your mother, Sandy. She was a delightful person. I'm so sorry for your loss."

Ren nodded his appreciation, unable to find the right words to answer her. She probably didn't mean anything by it, but every single person who brought up his mom talked about remembering her from childhood, as if they were intentionally avoiding her teenage years, when she'd left town. Even as nice as this Vi person seemed, there was a silent sort of judgment in that.

"I think you're going to like Bomont High," Reverend Moore said. "The graduating class is the biggest we've had in the school's history." He turned to a man in a standard blue blazer and gray pants who was hovering on the edge of the conversation, waiting to jump in. "How many seniors do we have this year?"

"A hundred and twenty," the man replied eagerly. "Give or take a dropout." That was maybe one quarter the size of the senior class at Ren's old school.

"Roger's the principal over at Bomont High," the reverend explained. That wasn't a surprise. The guy gave off a definite principal vibe.

It was the principal's turn to hold out his hand. Ren hadn't shaken this many hands in his life. "You start on Monday?"

"Yeah." Ren quickly adjusted when his uncle winced and shot him a warning glare. "Yes, sir."

"You got any problems, you come see me," the principal offered. "My door's always open." Ren couldn't imagine any problem he'd ever go to the principal for. He'd never even said so much as "hi" to the principal at his old school.

Roger gave him the once-over. "You play football?" he asked. "We could use a kicker." With Ren's slim body, he was never going to be a defensive lineman. "If you want to play for us, just stay clean and keep out of trouble. I heard you already had a run-in with the law."

That explained why he was hovering. The principal was also the town gossip. Ren hadn't planned on interacting much with the man before, and he was certainly going to avoid him now.

"You what?" Wes asked.

Ren hadn't thought to mention the ticket to his uncle. Seeing the expression on Wes's face, Ren realized he was going to have to do things differently while he lived under his roof.

It didn't help that Roger decided to twist the knife a little when he saw the surprise on Wes's face. "I don't know how it is up in Boston, but down here there's rules about playing your music too loud."

"Ren, you didn't tell me about—"

"And there's rules about tacky signage," Roger added. That seemed to be for Wes's benefit. "Don't mean to put on my councilman's cap here, Wes, but did you take that neon sign down yet? The one over your lot?"

"No," Wes said, silently stewing. "Not yet, Roger." Ren was glad that the attention had moved away from him, but Roger was still a major pain.

And he wouldn't stop. "It may sell cars, but it's against Code." Ren could hear the capital "C" when Roger said "Code."

A gentle hand took Ren by the arm. Vi pulled him away from the growing annoyance. "You don't want to listen to any of that, do you?" she asked.

"No. I mean, no'm." It still sounded weird. "Or, no, ma'am."

Vi laughed. "I didn't think so." She called out a name. "Ariel."

The girl who had been nonchalantly ignoring Ren turned at the sound of her name. She was a half second too slow in covering up her interest when she saw her mom walking over with Ren. At least that's how Ren read it. A crack was showing in her casual indifference.

"My daughter goes to Bomont High," Vi said. "You should have a friend on your first day. Ariel, this is Ren McCormack. He'll be attending school with you tomorrow."

A thousand witty greetings sprang to mind, but Ren settled on, "Hey."

"Hey," Ariel replied. Their eyes held on each other. It was an opening. Ren just needed to find something to say, but he didn't know what to talk about with this girl from a small town. Everything that came to him seemed so pretentious. What did they even have in common, beyond the fact that they both were trying to appear smoother than they probably were?

The moment passed when Ariel turned her attention over his shoulder. "Daddy? Rusty and I have that science project due tomorrow. We're going to head over to her house and work on it all night. I might just sleep over, if that's okay."

Ren didn't believe for a second this girl was worried about her homework. The tipoff was the vague "science project."

"On a school night?" her dad asked. "Is that really necessary?"

Without a beat, she turned and called to her friend. "Rusty? Don't you think it will take all night?"

The girl responded quickly. They'd either rehearsed this or done it before. "Sure. At least."

"I suppose it will be fine," the reverend said.

"Thanks, Daddy," Ariel said, all sweetness and light. "Bye, Mom."

Ren watched her walk off while trying not to look like he was watching. Maybe Bomont wouldn't be that bad after all.

Chapter 5

Ariel grabbed her bag out of the backseat of Rusty's car. Good thing her parents were gone before she left the house with it this morning; they might have figured out that her sudden overnight stay was planned in advance. She hadn't been completely sure it was going to happen when she'd packed the bag, but the text from Chuck confirmed that she'd need an excuse for staying out after curfew. Rusty's mom was much easier to get past on this kind of thing. Especially when she didn't know that Ariel was supposed to be at her house.

Actually, Rusty was the hard one to fool. She still worried about the little white lie even after they'd put miles between them and the church. It had been the first thing out of her mouth as soon as they were out of earshot of Ariel's parents. "He might be your daddy,"

Rusty had said, "but he's my preacher. I can't lie to a man of God. That's got to be a sin."

Ariel had relied on her go-to answer for these situations. "Only if you get caught."

It was true, in her mind. She had no problem separating her daddy from his job. His role in the town meant less and less to her after that night three years ago. His role as her father meant less every day, too.

"What do you think of the new guy?" Rusty asked as she drove down the two-lane blacktop that led them out of town.

"If you're into that kind of thing." Ariel shrugged. He was cute enough, but there was plenty of cute in Bomont. Didn't mean he was her type of guy.

There was that weird moment when she didn't know what to say to him, though. That didn't happen to her much around guys. Probably had to do with how she hated the trite things people said to her after Bobby's funeral. She'd heard her parents talking about how the Warnickers were expecting their nephew because his mom died. That was probably the only reason there was any awkwardness.

Ariel usually avoided anyone her parents introduced her to. It wasn't a good starting point for a relationship. She preferred the guys her parents didn't know a thing about.

Honestly, Ariel was more concerned with getting her tight jeans on underneath her dress at the moment.

There wasn't a lot of room to maneuver in Rusty's passenger seat.

"You mean guys my own age?" Rusty asked. "Yeah. I'm into that kinda thing." It was a dig at Ariel and the guy she was meeting. Chuck wasn't that much older than they were—just old enough that he could get her into the kinds of places guys in school couldn't.

When Ariel didn't answer, Rusty continued. "Well, I think he's sexier than all get-out. And he's from out of town, so don't tell me that doesn't curl your toes."

Those toes now slid into the flashy cowboy boots Ariel had ordered online. They were also the reason she'd gone with today's choice of nail polish. Her friend caught a glimpse of the red leather from the driver's seat. "Uh-oh," Rusty said. "Girlfriend's putting on her red boots. Ready to stomp your heart into the dirt."

That was the best thing about Rusty: she moved from mother hen to partner in crime without skipping a beat. As much as she liked to tell Ariel what to do sometimes, she also enjoyed the show.

Ariel didn't wear the boots for comfort. "My daddy hates these boots."

"I'm sure he's over the moon with them tight jeans."

"You can't wear skirts or dresses down on pit row," Ariel reminded her. Rusty knew better than that, but she rarely ever ventured beyond the stands at the racetrack. She watched with the other spectators, while Ariel preferred getting into the mix.

Ariel finished changing out of her churchgoing clothes and into her hell-raising ones. She dumped her bag in the backseat and topped off her look with some more makeup. She'd become an expert at applying while riding, adjusting for the bumps, the turns, and the hard, sudden stops that were Rusty's specialty.

Of course Daddy wouldn't like her in these colors. He'd hate everything down to the nail polish. "Painted like a harlot," he'd say. Or something like that. Ariel was a totally different person by the time they reached the racetrack, and not just on the outside.

Cranston Speedway was miles outside the Bomont town limits, and a whole world away from Ariel's regular life. It had a carnival atmosphere that extended to the parking lot—family entertainment mixed with something a little darker, a little seedier.

Excited fans cheered in the stands, where hot dogs and beer were the meal of choice, as bright-colored stock cars slid around each curve of the dirt track. This wasn't some nice, polished NASCAR event. This was down-and-dirty stock car racing. And the most down-and-dirty of the drivers was in the lead.

A car that Ariel was intimately familiar with broke away as the racers started the final lap. The driver's daddy may own the track, but he made a name for himself in the racing world in other ways. This race was no different. He cut off the lead car and pulled far ahead by the time the checkered flag dropped, the winner once again.

The announcer's crackling voice came over the shoddy PA system. "Today's stock car division two-time champion . . . folks, give it up for Chuck Cranston!"

Rusty cheered along with the crowd, but Ariel just watched in silence. Other girls would run straight over to the car, but she'd wait. Much as she wanted to tell herself that she was just being cool, the truth was, she didn't much care about the win. Chuck was always winning at something. He surrounded himself with friends who made sure his wins happened. She liked that "by any means necessary" aspect about him.

Chuck's admirers crowded around him as he stood on the roof of his car, flashing his devilish grin. Now that the spotlight was entirely on Chuck, it was time for Ariel to make her entrance.

She sauntered past the stands, feeling the warmth of the sun on her shoulders as she stepped out of the shade and into the sunlight. Chuck's eyes weren't the only ones on her as she approached the outer edge of the track.

He shouted something to her, but she couldn't hear him over the roar of the engines from the other cars still on the track. "What?" she yelled back.

"The flag!" he screamed, motioning toward the track official who had waved the checkered flag at the end of the race. "Bring me the flag, girl!"

Without a second thought, Ariel ran over to the official as he came down the ladder from his platform perched above the track. She snatched the flag before he realized what she was doing and hopped out onto the raceway.

The official shouted after her as she crossed the dirt track. "Hey! Get back here!"

Rusty screamed, too, but for different reasons. "Ariel! What the hell are you doing?"

Walking onto the track while the other cars took a final lap wasn't the smartest thing she'd ever done. But these were professional drivers. They were good at avoiding obstacles. Besides, they weren't even at race speed. Hardly more dangerous than crossing a busy street.

Ariel confidently sauntered along as the cars passed. Couldn't let Chuck see her sweat. The rednecks in the stands hooted and hollered, but their voices weren't nearly the loudest.

The track official screeched at her. "Young lady, you are not allowed on the track!" Like she cared.

"Get back here!" Rusty pled. "You're gonna get yourself killed out there!" The fear she heard in her friend's voice was the only thing that might have stopped her, but Ariel was committed now. It was just as dangerous to turn back as it was to proceed.

Another racer pulled off her helmet and hopped out of a car in pit row, adding to the chorus of voices. It was Caroline, who always seemed to be hanging around Chuck. "Get off the track, jailbait!" the trashy woman yelled. "Go back to Bomont and have a bake sale."

Ariel was in the pit now. She placed her middle finger on her eye, as if she was rubbing it. "Caroline, why is it every time you smile, I get dirt in my eye?" Juvenile? Yes. But Caroline made her go there sometimes. The woman threw herself at Chuck in the most pathetic ways, even when Ariel was around.

Chuck's cackle of laughter told Ariel that he appreciated the base humor. She climbed up onto the hood of his car for a kiss as the audience howled in approval. Didn't take much to win them over. Usually just a flash of her tight pants and red boots.

"Are you my trophy?" Chuck asked as they pulled apart.

"Not without a victory lap," she replied.

Chuck slid off the roof of the car, down into the window and the driver's seat. Ariel stuck her legs inside the window, resting them on his lap as she sat on the edge of the doorframe, half inside, half out. Chuck grabbed her legs and peeled out for his victory lap. The checkered flag, and Ariel's golden hair, flapped in the breeze.

The crowd ate it up as they tore around the track, but Ariel wasn't as into it herself. Sure, she was laughing and having fun, but it wasn't nearly as exciting as it could be. Chuck's arms squeezed too tightly onto her legs, and he hooted and hollered like they were doing something *truly* dangerous. He barely drove fast enough for her to get some truly good wind through her hair. This was nothing.

Ariel slammed her fist down on the roof, banging to get his attention. "I don't know how you win races with that candy-ass driving!"

"You want me to put the spurs to her?" he asked. "Hang on!"

Chuck held onto her legs tighter and revved his engine. Ariel knew goading him would work. Questioning Chuck's driving was like doubting his testosterone level. She grabbed onto the doorframe as her body jumped back when he stomped on the gas.

The cheers from the crowd changed to warning shouts, but Ariel didn't care. This was speed. This was *living*. This was the kind of driving that Bobby was doing before his death. This exhilaration was the last thing he experienced in life. Her fear now was nothing compared to her joy.

Chuck's car picked up speed every second, sliding sideways around each corner as the tires lost traction on the dirt track. "Faster!" Ariel screamed. "Come on! Faster!"

She never felt so alive. No one telling her what to do. How to dress. What music to listen to. It was just her and the car and the adrenaline. Even Chuck didn't matter anymore. Nothing did.

The final curve was coming up fast. Ariel held onto the window frame with all her might. What would happen if she let go now? Was Chuck holding her tight enough? Could he cling to her and steer at the same time?

The car spun out near the trailers, throwing Ariel's body against the doorframe. She slipped backward, but stayed upright. The jolt threw some fear into her, but Chuck never let go. Heart pounding, they came to a stop not that far from Rusty.

The expression on her friend's face slammed Ariel back into reality. Losing herself in that moment had clearly terrified Rusty. The girl didn't say a word. She just stomped off as Ariel hopped to the ground.

Rusty might complain at times, but she put up with a lot of her friend's crap. She was one of the few people who got to see the full Ariel these days. When even Rusty couldn't take it, Ariel knew she'd gone too far. She hurried after her friend, past the hoots and hollers from the crowd heading to the parking lot.

"Rusty!" she called out. "Rusty! Where are you going?"

Rusty spun on her. Eyes full of anger. "You know when you see on the news that someone got killed doing something stupid?"

Ariel rolled her eyes, trying to play it off. "Oh, great. This again." But Rusty had gotten to her. She hated seeing her friend look at her that way. Rusty was the one person she could count on these days to never let her down—even when Ariel did her best to disappoint Rusty.

"Well, I don't want to be the stupid friend who stands around watching," Rusty continued without hesitation. "He should never let you do that."

It wasn't fair to blame Chuck for Ariel's actions, but Rusty never liked him. She didn't like most of the guys Ariel hung around with these days. The problem was, when Ariel knew she should apologize, that was usually when her defenses went up and she found herself on the attack. She never understood why that happened. "So that's what you're going to do?" Ariel said. "You're just going to leave me?"

"*Me?* Leave *you?*" There were tears in Rusty's eyes. It made Ariel feel even worse. Rusty always took it hard when Ariel did these things, but it had never moved her to tears before.

Rusty's voice went uncomfortably soft. "I don't know what's going on with you anymore. Ever since Bobby . . ." Her voice trailed off. There was nothing more to say. She turned on her heel and walked away.

Ariel wanted to go after her. She wanted to hop in the car as Rusty got into the driver's seat. But what she'd said about Bobby hurt too much. Ariel couldn't sit beside Rusty on the long ride back to Bomont. Not right now. "Guess I'll get a ride back to town."

"I guess you will." Rusty peeled out of the gravel parking lot.

The crowd continued to head for their cars. Strangers pushed past Ariel on their way out. She didn't notice them. All she knew was that she was alone. But there was an easy remedy for that. She headed back to the track to find Chuck. He was always good for a distraction when she wanted to take her mind off everything.

Chuck Cranston may not be anyone's idea of a sparkling conversationalist, but she had Rusty for that . . . when Rusty was speaking to her. Chuck wasn't exactly the best boyfriend material, either. Much of their time together focused on him, not her. But he was always up for a good time and never took things too seriously. That was really all Ariel needed.

The only problem was that Chuck was much like his racecar; stuck on a single track. In some ways he was fun and exciting. But in other ways, Ariel knew being with him would never get her anywhere.

After the stands emptied and the other racers went off to their trailers or the bars, the only vehicle left on the track was the water truck spraying down the loose dirt. Ariel watched it make its lazy route from the back of Chuck's car trailer. With the door open, they had a semi-private room that was about as romantic as being in an open garage. Even so, Chuck tried to have his fun.

The hood of Chuck's car was still warm beneath Ariel's back as Chuck kissed her. His hands explored under her shirt, rubbing her soft belly in a circular motion. Each circle grew wider in a poor attempt at a smooth move. She gently pushed the hand away. "Why we gotta go so fast?"

"You looking for some choirboy to put a promise ring

on your finger?" Chuck's tone was playful, but something about the way he said it still bothered her. "You're not gonna get that with me, preacher's girl."

Ariel had been defined by her daddy's job since she was born. It only got worse when boys started noticing her. Anytime anyone used her daddy to describe her, it felt like an insult, whether it was or not. "I get that from everybody else. I'm not going to take it from you."

Chuck's face darkened. "So what do you want? Want to go steady? I could ask your daddy if we could go courtin'."

Ariel kind of liked the idea of bringing a race car driver a few years older than her to the house. She might have to use it someday when she got really mad at her parents. Chuck read her thoughts in her expression. "I doubt he knows about you and me, right?"

She didn't respond. Chuck already knew the answer. He clearly didn't care, either, because he started nuzzling on her neck instead of making more of a point out of it. "I thought it was real simple with you and me," he said. "I'm your man and you're my rebel child."

Ariel pulled away from him. "I'm not a child."

He refused to let it go. "Yeah? Prove it."

Ariel weakened under his stare. She should have gotten up and out of there. That would be the thing to do. Be strong. Always leave them wanting more.

But then what? Rusty had already left. Could she hitch a ride with one of the stragglers hanging around the track? That could be more dangerous than staying with Chuck.

Besides, part of her wanted this. It wasn't ideal, on top of a car in the back of a trailer. But it was more than she would have if she left. Then she'd be alone.

Her fingers found their way to the buttons of her top, popping them one by one as if her hands acted on their own.

But Ariel was in control. In total and complete control. Her stare met Chuck's. "Shut the door."

Chapter 6

Ren let out a frustrated groan. *Sometimes you just have to force things*. He wrapped his hands around the metal and gave a tug. Then another. Then a hard yank. The VW's door finally swung open with a moaning wail.

Success. He could now let passengers into the car without making them climb across the seat. He just needed to find some passengers.

Ren never expected to make a bunch of friends on his first full day in a new town. He hadn't even been to school yet. But something about the people he'd met so far confirmed every fear Ren had when he first stepped onto the bus that brought him to Bomont. He didn't want to be here.

He thought about getting emancipated before his mom died. He'd already been on his own most of the time. But where would he live? Some of his mom's debts had gone with her, but not all of them. He'd have had to start out with nothing. There was still a year of high school to deal with, so it wasn't like he could get a full-time job.

This had been his only choice, really. His mom made him see that before she passed. It wasn't that he didn't love his family, but he didn't really know them. Not well enough to be comfortable living in their home. Even the girls, who were great, were almost total strangers. That's why he'd spent most of the first two days in the garage working on the car. Conveniently, it needed a lot of work.

The VW didn't look like much, but it was his freedom in a town that had already punished him for listening to his music too loud. That was weird, but Ren tried not to let it bother him too much. The place would get better. It had to. If Ariel was any indication of what the rest of the town might have in store for him, then maybe there was a glimmer of hope.

Ren went into the house to say good night to his aunt and uncle, then returned to his room to clean up and get ready for sleep. He picked up the picture by his bed. It was one of his favorite photos of his mom, taken when her life was full of promise, before her illness took a sudden, dark turn.

He never remembered the bad times. The sick times. At least, he tried not to. This was the mom he imagined when he saw her. Full of life.

He put the picture back on the nightstand and got into bed, imagining her smiling face was looking down on him right now. Not that he really thought she was. He'd spent more time than most people his age wondering what happened after death, whether or not there was some great beyond. The jury was still out. He'd probably never come to a decision.

Light shined in on him after several hours of tossing and turning on the strange bed. A half hour later, he decided it was time to get up and face the day. And the town of Bomont.

Sarah and Amy were already halfway through their breakfast when Ren got to the table. They were dressed in the uniforms that were apparently mandatory in the elementary school. Lulu had made a point of letting Ren know the night before that he didn't have to worry about that at his school. Honestly, he hadn't even thought about it before she said anything. It wasn't like he was going to some private school.

"Morning, girls. What's on the menu?"

"Waffles!" Amy cheered.

"But I can make you whatever you want, Ren," Lulu quickly added from the kitchen. "I can make you an omelette, or eggs on toast—"

"Waffles would be great. Thanks!" Even when his mom had been at her healthiest, she was usually out the door to one of her two jobs before Ren got up. Waffles for breakfast on a school day was unheard of. To be able to choose something else if he wanted was almost unthinkable. Lulu probably just wanted to make him feel welcome. They couldn't possibly have breakfasts like this every day of the week.

Ren grabbed a seat beside Amy as Wes entered the kitchen. His littlest one was at full attention when she saw him. "Daddy, did you lift the toilet seat when you tinkled?"

"Yes, I did, Amy," Wes replied with a smile. "Thank you for asking."

"Did you put it down when you were done?" Sarah chimed in immediately.

Wes smiled like a man who's just been caught. "I will next time, darlin'. Daddy's late for work." He took a look at Ren. And then a second look at him. Ren wasn't sure what was wrong.

"You got jury duty?" Wes asked. Ren didn't know what his uncle was getting at, until he added, "What's with the tie?"

At that moment, all the females in the room chimed in, as if they were just waiting for a reason to bring it up.

"I like it," Sarah said.

"He looks handsome," Amy added.

Lulu put the plate of waffles in front of him. "I think he looks dashing. Ren, you can dress however you want."

Ren wasn't sure what they were talking about. He was just in regular school clothes: dark pants and a light green short-sleeve shirt. Okay, the tie might be a little out there for Bomont, but he'd worn it plenty of times at his old school. Ties weren't the norm in Boston public schools, either, but it wasn't nearly as odd as some of the things his friends used to wear.

"I had a skinny black tie just like that back in the day," Wes added. "Had piano keys running down the side."

"Those were his mullet days," Lulu added, as if it needed explanation.

Wes grabbed his wife around the waist, giving her a playful hug. "Those were my sexy days, baby. You should know, Miss Crimping Iron." Lulu gave him a light swat on the nose before he turned his attention back to his nephew. "Look, I'm just thinking about first impressions. That's all."

Ren wasn't sure what world he was in that a tie made for a bad first impression. He didn't look forward to finding out. He just swallowed his Yankee sarcasm and dug into his waffles.

Breakfast tasted even better than it looked, and it looked pretty good. Probably nobody in this town ever burned a meal or undercooked their eggs. They'd lose their membership in the Rotary Club or something. Not that Ren had a clue what a Rotary Club was, but he'd heard of them on old TV shows set in small towns like this.

· · · · ·

This morning, Rusty kept Ariel waiting, instead of the other way around. It was payback for yesterday, when

Ariel had slipped into her friend's house in the middle of the night. She and Chuck had their fun together and then went out for dinner. His version of wining and dining was beer and wings, but Ariel wasn't picky. The food wasn't half as good as her momma's traditional Sunday-night meatloaf, but the crazy bar he took her to beat the gloomy silence around the dining room table any day.

Chuck complained about having to drive her all the way back to Rusty's, revving his engine to let the entire block know he was there even though it was long after curfew. That was something she had to worry about, since she wasn't eighteen yet. Chuck didn't have that problem; he'd passed eighteen a few years ago. It was another one of the benefits of being with Chuck. Guys her age worried about junk like curfew and school nights way more than Ariel ever did.

Rusty's room was on the first floor, so getting in and out through the window was a lot easier than it would have been at Ariel's house. Rusty's mom didn't even know they had an overnight guest until she passed Ariel in the kitchen as she left for work.

"We're gonna be late for school," Ariel called through the closed bathroom door. Rusty had been in the shower an awfully long time. "Aren't you the one who usually cares about those things?"

"I got plenty of time," Rusty shouted back over the running water. "You're the one who's gonna get detention if you pick up another tardy slip."

Ariel leaned back against the door. Rusty was right. She was one note away from detention. Usually, she didn't mind staying after school—she got a lot of homework done that way. But the last time she was stuck in school she missed out on riding into Atlanta with Chuck. The only way to make sure that didn't happen again was by doing what she knew she had to do.

"Okay," Ariel said. "I'm *sorry*. I'm *sorry* I made a scene at the track. I'm *sorry* I caused you to worry. And I'm really, *really* sorry I tripped and fell on you when I climbed in the window last night."

The water stopped running. "That didn't sound very genuine."

"It sounds better when there isn't a door between us," Ariel said. She softened her tone. "But I really am sorry. And we really are late for school."

The door opened behind Ariel, nearly dropping her to the floor. When she turned, she was surprised to see that Rusty was already dressed, with her bag slung over her shoulder and a scowl on her face. "Fine," she said. "But we should really get going."

Ariel was torn between laughing and growling at her as they left for school. Rusty would let her get away with murder, but there always came a point where she made sure Ariel knew how lucky she was to have such an easygoing friend.

They arrived at school with plenty of time to get one of the good parking spots.

"Rah," Ariel cheered with sarcastic enthusiasm as they passed under the "Go Panthers" banner. It was their daily ritual, a fun way to take a swipe at school spirit. As if they cared about the football team.

Rusty was silent. Guess the apology wasn't quite fully accepted yet.

"Are you gonna pout all day?" Ariel asked. "I already said I was sorry."

Rusty finally relented, allowing the first smile of the day. It rarely took this long to get the girl to smile after they had a dustup, so it was especially nice to see. "It's Monday," Rusty said. "Everybody gets a do-over."

Ariel wasn't so sure she'd earned another do-over, but for the moment she was glad they could put it behind them. She would have said as much, but a strange sound drew her attention, along with the stares of everyone else in the student parking lot.

An old VW Bug rolled into the lot, with the stereo pumping a song Ariel didn't recognize. She'd never seen the car before either, but the person behind the wheel was somewhat familiar. It was the guy she'd met yesterday after church: Ren McCormack. She heard through the grapevine that he'd already gotten a ticket for a noise disturbance. Guess it didn't faze him much. Not enough to stop him from doing it again, anyway. Looked like Ariel wasn't the only one who could make an entrance.

Chapter 7

Maybe he should have disconnected his iPod from the tornado siren.

Ren expected a few turned heads when he pulled up to school, being the new kid and all. But the way every single student in the parking lot gaped at him like he just came down from the mother ship was a bit more attention than he had anticipated. Nobody stared that way when he drove up to his old school with the radio blaring; usually they just tuned to the station he was listening to and sang along. Yet another reminder he was a long way from home.

He went to public school in Boston. Not in the richest part of town, but the kids lucky enough to have cars there usually had models from this millennium. The Bomont High parking lot was filled with cars that had been around longer than their drivers. It almost went without saying that everyone who owned a car probably knew how to fix it; they'd have to if they wanted to keep it on the road. Ren was one of the few kids back home who had those skills.

Ren pushed open the driver's-side door and stepped out, giving everyone a better view of him. He tried to play it cool, but the stares were unnerving as he walked to the entrance.

In the sea of faces, the first one that stood out was the one he met the day before. Ariel seemed determined not to notice him, but her friend clearly wasn't in on the plan.

"That's a nice tie," the friend said as he passed. "I mean it. Don't let anyone tell you different."

Again with the tie . . .

Ren couldn't tell if she was being sarcastic or if she really meant it. She seemed friendly enough, bright and cheery, while Ariel continued to be cool and aloof. Ren stammered out a "Thanks," hoping he wasn't being grateful for an insult. He tried to remember the girl's name, but he couldn't. Ariel had said it yesterday when she needed someone to back up her lie. *Dusty, maybe?*

"Rusty," she said, providing her name with a warm smile that seemed genuine enough.

He nodded and looked to her friend. He definitely remembered her name, but didn't want to look like he did. "Ariel, right?"

"Very good." She casually turned away from him and walked away. Rusty was quick to follow.

Nice, Ren thought. Just enough disinterest to keep him interested. She might not know much about lying to adults, but she sure had practice messing with guys' minds. He was going to have to figure out some way to force her to really notice him one of these days. That kind of project could make this town a bit less boring.

The high school wasn't any more interesting than the rest of Bomont. It was a standard-issue redbrick building that looked exactly as Ren imagined it would.

Everyone stared at him inside the building, too. Some guys made fun of the tie. Girls whispered and giggled. He was prepared for the gossip, but this was ridiculous. He hadn't even done anything worth talking about yet. Didn't these people have more interesting things going on in their lives?

Probably not.

Ren passed a large window looking into the principal's office. Roger, the man he had met after church yesterday, was inside, trying to look casual as he kept an eye on every single student who passed. The name on the door was "Dunbar."

Ren pretended not to notice Principal Dunbar waving as he passed the window. The last thing he needed was for everyone to think they were old friends.

Since he just saw the principal, Ren figured the main office was nearby. He had to pick up his class schedule

and locker assignment, fill out all the proper paperwork, and other stuff. Preferably before the first bell rang.

A display case on the wall distracted him. A funeral
wreath hung behind the Plexiglas along with a framed
photo of five students. They were clearly close friends
by the way they hung all over one another as they posed
for the picture. The smiles on their faces were full of play-
fulness, like they all knew some secret joke the person
looking at the photo wasn't in on. The three guys wore
football uniforms. The girls were dressed casually. One of
them wore bright pink high-tops. A small plaque beneath
the wreath read, "You will not be missing from our lives."

That was it. No names. No explanation of what happened to them, why they were missing from anyone's
lives. It made sense, though. Anything that ended in the
deaths of five teens in a town this size wasn't something that needed to be explained. Everyone must've
known the story; only outsiders would need to be clued in.

Ren pushed the dark message from his mind and
turned down the hall, walking right into a big, beefy guy
who was all arms and gangly body. "Hey, why don't you
watch where you're goin'?" He had the thickest south-
ern accent Ren had ever heard.

"I'm sorry." Ren's brain was still a bit rattled from
the collision. "I just didn't—"

"It's like driving," the guy said, cutting him off. "Keep
to the right side of the hallway."

Okay, now Ren's brain was functioning again. He

wasn't going to let some rube in a camouflage shirt and trucker hat think he was the one who didn't know how to walk. "You're kinda hard to see with all that camo. Aren't you supposed to wear one of those orange vests so hunters don't shoot you?"

"I wouldn't be caught dead wearing orange," he said. "I ain't no Tennessee Vols fan. I'm a Georgia Bulldog, head to toe." It was like he was speaking a different language, and not just because of the accent. "Where you from?" he asked. "You talk funny."

Ren let out a snort of laughter. Something about a pot and a kettle came to mind. "*I* talk funny? You should hear you from my end."

Uncle Wes probably would have warned him to dial back the sarcasm. *Don't want to make for a bad first impression.* But Ren wasn't really worried about impressing this young man. "Boston," he said, answering the guy's question. "Massachusetts. It's in the United States."

"Yeah, I read that somewhere." The big guy's hand shot out. For a brief moment Ren though he was about to get a punch for his troubles, but the smile that came with the extended hand said otherwise. "I'm Willard."

Ren shook Willard's hand and introduced himself. "Ren McCormack."

"Anybody give you grief about that tie yet?" Willard asked.

Only everyone. But Willard didn't need to know that. "Well, the day just started," Ren said.

Things looked up for a bit after that. Willard directed Ren to the main office, then went along with him to make sure he made it there safely. The guy had a bit of a puppy-dog quality, and spent the rest of the morning following Ren around school. Since they had pretty much the same schedule, it made sense. The school wasn't big enough to get lost in, but Willard saved him from making a few wrong turns between classes.

By the time they got to gym class, Ren had a good idea on the layout of the place. He quickly changed in the locker room and headed outside with the rest of the class. They were doing track and field, but it wasn't an organized activity in any way that Ren could see.

Halfway through the period, it was Ren's turn to step up to the starting line at the track. Willard was beside him. The gym teacher, Coach Guerntz, barked out orders as they took their starting positions. "Keep that head down. Keep it down! All the way! Good. Next group, on your mark, and . . . Go!"

Ren took off, leaving Willard and the others in the dust. It was just a short sprint, but it felt good to get his blood pumping again. He didn't need the coach to tell him how fast he was. The eyes that followed him down the track finally had something interesting to watch. He easily won the sprint and a few smiles of approval from a group of nearby girls. Too bad Ariel wasn't among them.

He'd seen her a few times that morning. They had a couple classes together. Each time they passed, she was either deep in conversation with Rusty or off in her own world. The way she barely noticed him made Ren wonder if he completely imagined that awkward moment they shared at church. Maybe it didn't mean anything at all. Maybe it was just . . . awkward.

Ren lined up with bunch of other guys at the water hose that served as the makeshift fountain. He waited his turn as the coach shouted out needless orders on the proper way to take a cold drink when exercising. This had to be his thing, a way to exert control by explaining how the students should do everything.

The kid finishing up at the hose handed it to Willard. "You look a little flushed, Willard."

"My cheeks are naturally ruddy," he said between panting breaths. The sprint had taken a bit out of him. He looked much paler now, especially when compared to the darker skin of the guy handing him the water hose. "Ren, this is Woody, our team captain. But you don't gotta salute him."

Ren held out a hand. "Good to meet you."

Woody joined up with them as they made their way through the different stations the gym coach had set for the students. The class wasn't much more than random exercises while Coach bellowed about nothing at all. It did leave plenty of time for talking, so Ren didn't mind. Especially since the talk was mostly about him.

"You keep running that fast, Coach Guerntz is gonna

be on you to sign up for football," Woody said. They stood at the row of metal pull-up bars sticking out of the ground. Willard was halfway through a set.

Ren had been afraid of something like that happening when he decided not to hold back in gym class. He fielded offers to join other sports teams all the time back at his old school, as if the coaches back there didn't realize he was already involved in a sport. "That's not really my thing."

Willard dropped down from the pull-up bar. "Not much else to do in this town as far as sports or extracurricular is concerned."

Ren took his place at the bar and ran through a series of fast pull-ups. He knew he should slow down, not show off. But he hadn't had a real workout in weeks. It felt good to get the muscles moving again.

"Shit-howdy," Willard said.

Ren skipped a beat in his pull-ups and nearly slipped off the bar. "Shit-howdy" was a new one to him. He didn't even want to know how Willard came up with it.

"You say you're not into sports?" Woody asked.

Ren held himself up on the bar, with his arms straight. "I didn't say that. I'm just not into football."

Willard seemed confused. In his world, there probably wasn't any sport other than football. "Then what are you—"

Ren cut him off by lifting his legs and throwing

himself into a loop that took him up and over the metal bar, giving them a quick glimpse of his high bar routine. He stopped to hang in midair, enjoying the gasps of surprise from Willard and Woody.

"I was on the gymnastics team at my school," Ren explained. "Won the regionals. Got a couple trophies. No big whoop."

Three guys over at the next pull-up station were watching him, too. They didn't seem the least bit impressed. "If you want, they got a balance beam for the cheerleaders to practice on," one of them said.

Another added his two cents. "Yeah. They could give you a baton and you can twirl all day long."

Ren hopped down from the bar. He'd heard plenty of that kind of thing since he started gymnastics. Nothing new. He had loads of experience handling it himself, but Willard was already moving toward the guys threateningly. This was not going to go well for Willard.

The third guy stepped in before things went too far. "Now, now, Willard. You don't want to get suspended again. Your momma might have to take a switch to you."

The trio walked away while Willard remained in place, stewing.

Ren whispered to Woody. "What'd he get suspended for?"

"Fightin'."

Willard turned back to them with a hint of a smile

that indicated he wasn't embarrassed by the suspension. "I've been known to open a can." Willard didn't look like he'd be much in a fight, but Ren knew plenty of guys much smaller than Willard who were good in a scrape.

The near-fight went completely unnoticed by the coach, who was busy telling a group of students about the proper way to do cool-down exercises. He eventually gave up and dismissed everyone back to the locker room to change.

Lunch was next. Ren got into the serving line with Willard. He was glad to avoid the awkward maneuver of figuring out where to sit on the first day. They went outside to the courtyard as Willard went on about his favorite subject: football.

"Last year, the varsity team made it all the way to regionals. They bused us down for that one. The excitement never stops." Willard held up his thumbs in mock enthusiasm, once he put down his tray.

Ren sat across from him. "You ever been overseas?"

"I been to Alabama. That count?"

"Not really," Ren replied. Although down here it probably did. "Two years ago, I went to Russia with my gymnastics team. Kind of this sister-city thing with Moscow."

"I don't know if I'd dig that," Willard said. "Seems like it'd be boring."

Ren smiled. Time for some fun. "Do you know anything about Russian girls?"

"I hear they range from scary to drop-dead beautiful."

"Well, I can vouch for the latter." Ren saw that he had Willard's full attention. "Two girls from the Russian gymnastics team snuck me out of my dorm in the middle of the night. And they were smokin'."

"What were they smokin'?" Willard looked confused. "Oh, you mean like 'smokin' hot'? Please continue."

"We go to this club and the music is pounding. They must have had like three smoke machines going, 'cause you couldn't see a thing. We were all over each other, drenched in sweat. It was great. We danced all night."

Willard leaned forward in his seat. "And then what? What happened after that?"

Ren shrugged and gave him a little smirk. That was pretty much the whole story, but Willard didn't need to know that. The big guy didn't seem at all content with that response. "Down here in the South we don't start stories like that and not finish."

Well, okay, if it was a story he wanted, Ren was happy to provide. He leaned forward, too, as if he didn't want anyone else to hear. This was all for Willard's benefit. "Well, it goes without saying that they were both very flexible." From there, Ren composed a tale that would make a football player blush—literally. Willard was rapt with attention through the whole racy story, until the point he realized it was all a joke.

"Aw, man," Willard said. "No fair. You got me all excited and you didn't even get nowhere with them."

"But we did dance," Ren added wistfully. "We danced our asses off."

Chapter 8

Andy Beamis seemed like a fair enough guy. He took one look at Ren when he pulled up to the Beamis Cotton Mill, tilted his head in a way that said, "I can work with this," and started showing him around the place. Ren figured Andy must be really good friends with Wes, because that was the only thing that could explain why he'd even remotely consider hiring someone so clearly out of his element.

"You know how to operate pallet jacks?" Andy asked.

"Uh-uh." He didn't even know what a pallet jack was.

"Can you work a stitching pedal?"

"I don't know," Ren admitted. "Never seen one."

Andy paused, as if he were rethinking this whole arrangement. "Where'd you say you were from?"

"Boston, Mass."

Andy nodded. "Did they teach you anything useful up north?"

"Just enough to get by," Ren said. "But I'm hoping y'all could teach me the three Rs."

"The three Rs?"

Ren threw on an accent heavier than Willard's. "Readin', writin', and redneckery."

This time the pause was a bit longer than the last. Ren feared he had gone too far, showed a bit too much of that Yankee sarcasm. It wasn't the best way to treat a potential boss. Andy's face cracked into a slow, knowing smile. "People been givin' you a hard time?"

Ren nodded. School had been good enough thanks to Willard, but that didn't mean anyone else was welcoming him with open arms. The whispers and stares followed him around town for the first couple days, like everyone expected him to do something wrong. It certainly didn't help that Bomont had its own crazy quirks.

How was Ren supposed to know that the seniors had an extremely limited reading list? He'd picked *Slaughterhouse-Five* as his choice for his first report in English class and the teacher went ballistic, telling him he couldn't read that trash in the classroom. The next three books he chose were denied as well, which was ridiculous. The main reason he'd thought of them was because he'd already read them for school years ago. It was like some of the rules were there just to make strangers feel like outsiders no matter what they did.

"I can see that," Andy said. "You're young. From out of town. You're a smart aleck."

Well, that was that. Maybe he should have taken Wes seriously about his sarcasm.

"Can you start Thursday?" Andy asked.

The question caught him off guard. "Yes. Yes, sir."

Andy clapped his hand on Ren's shoulder. "I'll help you with the reading and writing. You're on your own with the redneckery."

Oh, but Ren had plenty of help with that as he made his way through the town over the following week. Bomont was a different kind of place than Boston, and not just because it was smaller. The people were different. The food was different. Even the activities were different.

Weekly attendance at church was now mandatory. It was a non-negotiable point with his uncle and aunt. It wasn't like the hour he gave up for it was the end of the world or anything, but the reverend's sermons were beginning to feel frozen in time, stuck in an age when people griped about anything new or different. Being the most new and different thing in town, Ren couldn't help but take it personally, though he was aware that the preacher didn't mean it that way.

Ren knew he wasn't giving the place a fair shake, but the townsfolk weren't being all that welcoming to him, either. Aside from Willard and Woody, he hadn't made any friends in his first couple weeks. Ariel continued to ignore him, and no other girls at school had sparked his interest the way she did. He knew she was playing games by ignoring him, but it still got to him.

The guys came over to help with the car after church. It was moving along well enough with all the changes he'd made over the past couple weeks, but it wouldn't hurt any to see if they could get it to run a little quieter. He'd only get in more trouble if he tried to drown out the noise with his music.

There was something that Ren wanted to talk about, but he didn't want to sound too eager to discuss it. "So what's the story with the preacher's daughter?" he asked, as if he really couldn't care less. If Ariel could do it, he could, too. "Every time I talk to her, she brushes me off."

Woody wiped some grease off his forehead. "Back in the day, she used to be a Goody Two-shoes. Now she's frontin' like she's some hell-raiser. Wears her jeans all tight . . ."

"You could put a quarter in her back pocket and tell if it's heads or tails," Willard added, sounding like a man with some experience looking at her back pocket.

Ren shrugged it off so they didn't get the wrong idea. Or the right one. "I was just curious. It's not like I was going to take her out dancing."

Willard laughed like Ren had just made a joke. "That'd be pretty hard, being that it's illegal."

"What? Dating a preacher's daughter?" This was a very, very strange town indeed.

"Public dancing is against the law," Woody said.

"Jump back." It was even stranger than Ren imagined.

"It's been that way for three years," Willard said.

They had to be joking. Messing with the new kid. But the looks on their faces told Ren they weren't making this up. "You're serious about this? You mean Bomont High doesn't have school dances?" That didn't make any sense. How could an entire town agree not to dance?

"There's what they call the Fall Ball," Willard explained. The way he said it made it sound like it wasn't much of a party. "That's held at the church. The whole town shows up. Everybody's eyes on you. And for one song they make you dance with your mother."

That last part didn't sound so bad to Ren, but the rest of it was not his idea of fun.

"The schools don't want to have dances on their property," Woody added. "They don't want to be held liable."

"Liable for what?" Ren asked.

Willard shrugged. "Not much to do in a small town after a dance except get drunk or get pregnant."

"Or get killed," Woody threw in with all seriousness. "That's what started this whole thing. Five seniors got killed at this kegger party after a homecoming game. That's when the whole town went crazy, blaming it on the liquor, the music, the dancing. Pretty soon everybody started thinkin' dancing was a sin."

That explained the memorial in the middle of the school hallway. Ren had walked by it plenty of times since his first day, but he never thought to ask anyone what it was all about. It seemed obvious enough that the teens had been in some tragic accident. He never guessed that it had led to something like this.

"A sin?" Ren asked. "We're talking about the law, not Heaven and Hell."

Willard nodded. "Take it up with Reverend Moore."

Ren didn't imagine that happening anytime soon.

Chapter 9

After a few weeks of being ignored, Ren was about to give up on Ariel entirely. But old habits must die hard, because somehow his hand just had to wave to her one last time as he and Willard left school on Friday afternoon.

He nearly tripped over his own feet when she waved back. *Okay, play it cool.* Now that the door was open, he wanted to go over and say hi to her, but he didn't want to push his luck. Better to just leave it at a wave and hope for more next time.

The rumble of an engine behind him clued him in to his mistake. Ariel wasn't waving at him. She was waving at the driver of the oversize truck pulling into the parking lot.

The guy behind the wheel was even louder than his

engine when he called out to her. "Afternoon, little school girl. Hop in. You can tell me all about algebra."

Ren watched Ariel slide into the truck. Then, to make the whole thing worse, the guys that had given him grief in gym class on his first day piled into the back. Since that day, Rich, Russell, and Travis hadn't exactly made their hatred of him secret. Ren didn't know what he did to earn their attention, but they had already had some minor run-ins. The ape in the driver's seat was still a mystery, though.

"There he goes, right there!" Rich yelled out, pointing frantically at Ren, so there wasn't any mistake who he was talking about.

"Where's your tie, big shot?" the driver yelled.

Seriously? His tie was still that big a talking point? He hadn't worn it since the first day. Ren ignored the guy as he and Willard got into the VW.

"Great," Willard said. "It's Upchuck."

"Didn't you hear?" Russell yelled, making a big show of it for everyone heading to their cars. "He's a big star in gymnastics."

Great. That stuck, too. Ren hadn't done any gymnastics moves since the first gym class, either. These guys had long memories for such tiny brains.

Chuck picked up on the comment. "Gymnastics? Where I come from, the only people into gymnastics are girls and fags. Which one are you?"

87

Ren couldn't let that one go. "Yeah? Well, where I come from, the only people who still use the word 'fag' are inbreds or assholes. You just might be both." He ended the conversation by hitting the gas and pulling out, but not before he was rewarded with the wonderful sound of Ariel's laughter. Too bad Chuck cut it off quickly with a withering glare.

Willard directed Ren out of town to an old, abandoned scrap yard where they hoped to find a few parts for the Bug. It ran pretty well now, but Ren wanted some spare parts on hand in case of emergency. This was a high-maintenance vehicle. Willard figured they should be able to scrounge some random junk in the automobile graveyard.

Ren's mind wasn't on his car as they walked between the stacks of rusty metal. "Tell me about this Chuck guy," he said to Willard. "What's Ariel doing with him, anyway?"

"He's your typical born-with-a-silver-spoon-in-his-mouth bad seed," Willard said. "Every town has one."

Yeah," Ren agreed. "We had plenty back home." That was one thing he couldn't blame on Bomont. Jackasses were universal.

"Rusty says that Ariel's just acting out," Willard said. "That Chuck is some kind of phase."

Ren picked up on the meaningful way his friend said Rusty's name. That girl was the one bright spot in his plan to get Ariel's attention. Every time Ariel ignored him,

Rusty was there to respond for her, loudly, to make sure he knew they both noticed him. Now it seemed like Willard was doing some noticing on his own.

"Oh?" Ren slapped Willard's arm. "Rusty said this? You two talk about things much?"

Willard revealed a shy smile. "Well, it's a small town. Ain't that many people to talk to. I've known Rusty for years."

"Uh-huh?" Ren said. "What's that you say about starting stories and not finishing them?"

"No story to tell," Willard said. "And I ain't makin' one up for your entertainment. It'd be disrespectful."

Ren laughed. Ever the gentleman. "Okay, okay, but I didn't ask you to."

A rusted side-view mirror came off in Willard's hand when he touched the burned-out hulk beside him. "What are we doin' here again?"

"Beats me," Ren said, looking over the junk. Most of this stuff was useless to him. "It was your idea."

Willard's face lit up. "Well, I just got me a better one. Come on."

They raced back to Ren's car, and Willard guided them out of the scrap yard and back through the streets of Bomont till they reached the Starlite Drive-in. Ren wasn't really in the mood for a movie, but it didn't matter when he saw the big gash in the screen.

"They ain't showed movies here in years," Willard said. "But the diner serves the best barbecue in town."

The Grill was packed for an early Friday night, but everyone was way too quiet. Nobody seemed to be having any fun. That probably had something to do with Officer Herb keeping watch over the place as he leaned against his cruiser, eating a corndog.

"See you first thing next week, McCormack," Herb said through a mouthful of food when the guys passed.

Ren answered Willard's unasked question. "I gotta go to traffic court."

"For what?" Willard asked.

The Bug could still barely make the speed limit half the time, so it was a logical question. "Listening to Quiet Riot."

"Who?"

Ren wasn't sure if Willard was messing with him by acting like he'd never heard of Quiet Riot, or if he truly meant it. It made perfect sense that his friend wouldn't have had any exposure to the classics in a town where no one was allowed to have fun.

The diner was crowded with as many teens inside as there were in the parking lot, probably because it was one of the few places in town where adults weren't out in force. It was just enough of a greasy spoon to keep anyone with better dining options away, but not so gross that Ren wouldn't eat there. Woody was in line at the counter with his girlfriend, Etta. He waved when he saw Ren. "What's up, McCormack? You hungry?"

"What's good?" Ren asked. The menu had the basics: burgers, fries, and an unhealthy selection of barbecued meat. There were also some foreign food items that Ren couldn't begin to understand. "Foreign" was defined as anything he wouldn't see on a menu back in Boston.

The nervous smile on Willard's face made more sense when Ren saw Rusty walking up to them with a paper bowl filled with what looked to be Fritos drowning in cheese and some kind of meat. Ren didn't think Willard's dumb grin had anything to do with the food. "Frito Pie, all the way," she said. "And if you're a man, you'll put some jalapeños on that."

Ren couldn't imagine any of the girls he knew back home eating that junk, but Rusty didn't hesitate. Like she could care less what anyone thought about her dining habits. Ren scooped up a cheesy Frito and tossed it into his mouth. *Not bad.*

Willard didn't have as much luck. Rusty pulled her food away when he went in for some. "Get your fingers out of my pie." The smile she gave him told Ren that Rusty had learned some lessons from her friend about playing hard to get with guys. Or maybe she knew enough about the subject without anybody's help. The way Willard looked at her, she seemed to be doing fine without Ariel around.

Willard pointed at Ren. "What about that guy? You don't know where his finger's been."

She responded by putting another Frito on her tongue. She did it so playfully that Ren had to laugh. She was actually a lot of fun on her own.

A now-familiar rumble shook the diner, and heads turned toward the parking lot. Ariel still rode shotgun in Chuck's truck with the trio of losers in the back.

"Thought Ariel was coming with you," Etta said to Rusty.

"Yeah, well, Ariel's got her own plans. I just haven't been a part of them." Rusty turned to Ren. "What do you do when the people you love let you down?"

"Don't get me started," Ren replied.

A whistle from the kitchen got everyone's attention. The cook called out from the back. "Woody! Woody! Check your six, man."

Woody's eyes went straight for Officer Herb's police cruiser as it pulled past Chuck and out of the parking lot. "Five-O is getting his move on. Whatcha got, Claude?"

The cook, Claude, held up a CD. "David Banner bootleg. But look-it—don't get too drunk out there. First sign of the po-po and I pull the plug. Two at a time, Woody."

That was an odd order. Ren looked to Willard for clarification. "What's he mean, 'two at a time'?"

"You personally get fined if you're dancing in a lewd or lascivious manner," Willard said, slurring the word "lascivious" in a way that made it difficult for Ren to understand at first. "But if there's three or more they can fine the drive-in for holding an unauthorized dance."

This no-dancing rule kept getting more and more ridiculous. "I thought everybody in these red states didn't like government interfering in their lives," Ren said.

"Now, don't you get *me* started," Rusty said as she threw the rest of her Frito Pie in the trash and moved toward the door.

Claude took down the PA microphone for pick-up orders and pointed it at his grease-covered boom box. He slapped in the CD and the air filled with lewd and lascivious music. It was a classic song, pumped up with a modern beat.

All food was forgotten as Woody took charge. He led everyone out to the lot, where the cars were already pulling into a circle so their headlights could light an improvised dance floor. They didn't waste any time moving into position, like everyone was just waiting for Officer Herb to leave.

"Hey, Woody," Claude called out one more time. "No po-po, man."

"Woody and everyone get all *Mad Max Beyond Thunderdome* out here," Willard explained. Ren wasn't sure what that meant, but he was about to find out.

It started with Woody moving into the circle of light and letting the music flow through his body. His moves were raw, but smooth. Rocks kicked up and dust flew as he slid up to another guy like a dare.

The two of them moved in a back-and-forth dance battle, each trying to one-up the other. The moves were frantic with energy, quick and hard. This was street dancing. Their moves came from the music; it wasn't anything they learned in a class. But they were good. *Damn good.*

"Can you believe that's our linebacker?" Willard asked.

That was almost the least surprising part.

The music surrounded Ren. It wasn't just coming out of the PA, it was in all the broken-down old drive-in speakers as well. Claude probably put some money into keeping them on, which said a lot about the way he felt about the ban on music.

A third dancer jumped into the mix. Everyone around the dirt dance floor hooted and hollered like police sirens. They celebrated the absurdity of the law, showing no respect for the letter of it. A squeal of feedback broke in before Claude's voice came over the PA. "Hey! You cut that out! I'm gonna turn it off if this gets too rowdy!"

The three dancers jumped out of the circle, tagging in two others to take their places. Everyone had his own style of dancing. Nothing formal, not always smooth— like they didn't get the chance to do this too often. Most of these moves were learned in tiny bedrooms, banging around listening to the music on headphones so their parents didn't know what they were up to. Still, some of the dancers impressed Ren more than the kids back home who took this kind of freedom for granted.

Ariel stood in the back of Chuck's truck bed, putting

94

on some kind of show. It looked like she was doing ballet positions, so far as Ren could tell. There'd been a ballet class after gymnastics at the Y when he was a kid; sometimes he stuck around to watch, and recognized first and second position from that. Ariel held pretty steady, balancing on the truck. She must have studied for years.

Her denim jacket came off, and the dancing turned from a poised ballet to something slow and seductive. The music dulled in his ears as his eyes focused on her body. The way she moved. It almost made him forget they were in public. He wanted to go to her. To move with her.

But then her dance took on more of a stripper vibe as Chuck sat back and watched. His friends were watching, too. Practically drooling. Ren wouldn't have been surprised if one of them took out a dollar bill and held it up in the air. The show was getting uncomfortable, and Ren wasn't the only one that noticed.

"What the hell is she doing?" Rusty asked. Her voice was full of concern mixed with anger.

"Losing her damn mind," Etta replied.

Ariel spun and grinded to the music on the flatbed truck, then jumped down in between two girls dancing in the circle. The crowd went wild with siren sounds and other, dirtier noises as the girls moved with the music.

It was like she fired a starting pistol, signaling it was time to go crazy. Everyone jumped into the circle, moving with wild abandon. Rusty forgot about her friend's behavior and bounced on her heels to the music. Etta and Woody moved in unison, their bodies fitting together like they'd danced this way before. Only Willard hung back, but Ren wasn't about to stay on the sidelines with him.

Ren started out at the edges along with everyone else, but quickly worked his way into the center, moving closer to Ariel. This time when he caught her eye, he could tell that she definitely noticed. He kicked his dancing up a notch, hoping to keep his audience.

The warning squawk of Claude's PA was enough to send almost everyone scattering back to their cars. Ren was glad to see that Ariel had stayed out there with him. They danced separately at first, as if everyone else was still on the dance floor. If she was going to ignore him, he'd do the same to her. It was enough to be near her for now.

Ren lost himself in the music, forgetting for just a moment that this hot girl was beside him. That changed when he saw that he had her full attention for the first time since he'd met her. The dancing did it. The moves he had. That was the thing she couldn't ignore. For the moment, she was his.

He pulled out his best tricks, mixing dance with gymnastics, climbing up onto a big four-wheel-drive truck and doing a back flip off the hood. The alarm went off as the blue truck rocked, adding a new sound to the music.

"Aw, dude, I'm sorry about that," Ren said to the big guy who owned the truck.

"No worries," he said as he silenced the alarm. "Do it again."

Ren didn't have to be told twice. He hopped up onto the truck and did another back flip, arcing even higher in the air than the last time. When he landed, he slapped hands with the truck owner and asked if Ariel was still watching.

"Oh, she's looking," the guy said. "Get on that, boy."

Ren ran and slid up to Ariel with amazing force, nearly knocking himself off his feet. The move forced her up against the grille of a car. If there was any doubt about the attraction between them, it was now gone.

"Hey," Ariel said in a soft voice that somehow managed to drown out the loud music.

"Hey," Ren replied.

"Ren, right?"

He smiled. "Very good."

They danced together, moving seductively to the music. Ren was enjoying himself for the first time since moving to Bomont. And it wasn't just because this beautiful girl paid more attention to him dancing than she did in the halls at school—though that was a big part of it. Still, he still didn't have her entirely. She kept looking over her shoulder, glancing back to Chuck. With each turn, she moved a little closer to Ren. Danced a bit dirtier.

Ren could see that Chuck was getting jealous. *Good. Let him.* Ren was having fun in the moment. But Ariel's glances back happened more and more often, until her focus was almost entirely on watching Chuck's face darken with anger. It was too much for Ren. He stopped dancing, which brought her attention fully back to him.

Ariel kept moving provocatively. "What's wrong? Can't keep up?"

"You can put on a show for that guy," Ren said. "Doesn't mean I got to."

"Hey—" Ariel said, but she never got to finish.

The music broke off suddenly, bringing the party to a screeching halt. Claude's voice came over the PA. "Attention. Would Ariel please come up to the diner? Your daddy's here for you, Ariel."

Everyone turned to see Reverend Moore standing in the doorway.

The crowd reacted for their friend's sake. Rusty was especially mortified. Her gasp was the only thing that could be heard in the sudden silence.

Ren caught a blip of concern in her eyes, but Ariel remained stone-faced through it all. "Show's over," she said to Ren before abandoning the dance floor and heading for the diner.

The air that had been electrified with music a moment earlier was now quiet as death while the crowd parted for Ariel to make her way to her father. Their private conversation was all that could be heard.

"Your mother didn't think you had any money on you," Reverend Moore said. "She told me this is where you'd be."

"Daddy, I wasn't—"

"I think it would be best if you came home with me," the reverend said. "Right now."

The silence continued as all eyes followed Ariel and her father while they walked to his car. Ren saw her glance Chuck's way. The jerk seemed amused by it all, making a "call me" sign with his hands. Not out of concern—like he wanted to plan their next date.

Once they were both in the car with the door shut, it was the signal for everyone to start whispering about what they'd just seen.

"Ouch," Willard said. "Daddy's gonna take her out to the woodshed."

"What the hell does that mean?" Ren asked.

"It means she's in trouble."

They both looked across the lot at Chuck. He was already eyeing other girls in the crowd. When he saw them looking his way, he lifted a beer and smiled as if nothing at all had just happened.

Chapter 10

Ariel discreetly checked behind her in the side-view mirror. The silence in the dance circle broke the moment Daddy pulled his door shut. He didn't slam it; that wouldn't be very mature. For all the conversations now going on behind them, it was eerily quiet in her father's sedan.

Before they pulled onto the road, Ariel was already the talk of the town. That wasn't anything new. She'd set tongues wagging for years now. At least this was for something she'd actually done.

But what had she done, really? She had danced. That was it. She wasn't even dancing with her boyfriend. It was just some random guy. The random guy her mother introduced her to, in fact. That was something she might want to hold in reserve, should she ever need to use it.

Ren McCormack had been taking up more of her thoughts lately than he should. Sure, she pretended that she couldn't remember his name, that she barely noticed him in the halls; but there was something about him that attracted her. He wasn't like the other guys that caught her eye—and it had nothing to do with the fact that he was from out of town.

He didn't hesitate for a second calling her out when he caught her checking back to make sure Chuck was watching. Anyone else might have noticed that, but he was the only one to say it. And he stopped dancing, too. Most guys would have played it up, even the ones dumb enough to know how mad it would make Chuck. It was all worth it for a twirl with the preacher's baby girl.

Daddy carefully drove through town at his usual speed, just under the limit. Nobody was going to pull over the reverend, but the reverend would never flout the laws he so carefully worked to maintain as a council member and the moral leader of the community. Funny how she was almost the immoral leader of the community.

Of course, Ariel wasn't the one who turned on the music in the first place. She didn't start the dance—but she was the one who got caught. It actually worked out for the best, really; because she was the one who ultimately didn't mind what happened to her.

Not really.

Mostly.

The house was dark when they drove up to it. There was only one light on in the living room window. Reverend Moore pulled into the driveway and turned off the ignition, but he didn't move to get out of the car. Ariel didn't, either. They just sat in silence, each waiting for the other one to give in.

As Ariel expected, it was her father who broke first, though he couldn't quite bring himself to look at her. "You know, Ariel, I cannot be with you at all times to protect and guide you. The manner in which you were dancing was beneath you. Why you choose to celebrate such vulgar music is beyond me."

It was like he totally forgot what it was to be young. "Didn't you ever dance with Mom?"

"Of course I did." He turned in his seat to face her. "But every time I did, I looked her in the eye. I treated her with respect. These days, 'dancing' means young girls sticking their backsides into boys' crotches. And when they dance like that, they become sexually irresponsible."

It was the same stupid logic he always used. The idea that dancing led to sex. People were having sex without any musical accompaniment since Adam and Eve. Ariel was over that argument long ago. "Can we just get on with whatever judgment you want to dole out? Am I grounded? Do I gotta go to prison? What is it?"

Moore shook his head as if he'd given up on her. That hurt more than anything he could say, more than any punishment he could give. "Ariel, I just don't know what I'm going to do with you."

"There's nothing to do, Daddy. This is it. It doesn't get much better." She pushed the car door open and got out.

Her father called after her to stay in the car, but she didn't care. He wasted the entire ride not speaking to her. She wasn't about to cause a scene in the driveway while her mother sat inside the house thinking everything was perfect.

Nothing had been perfect in Ariel's life since that night three years ago. Nothing at all.

Ariel stormed into the house. Her mom sat on the sofa reading, totally unaware of the coming storm. "Hey, baby," she said innocently. "You're back early. What did you do tonight?"

"Just breaking the law, Momma." Ariel stormed off to her bedroom.

Her father called after her. "Ariel, we're not done—"

She slammed her bedroom door to let him know that she was most certainly done. But it wasn't enough. She wanted to slam every door in the house. She wanted to smash things. Destroy the perfect family portrait on her desk. Stomp on the little unicorn music box Daddy gave her on her eighth birthday. But that would only prove him right, that she was a child. That she wasn't mature enough to dance without it leading to trouble.

Instead, she threw her body down on her bed and listened to her parents' muffled voices from the living room. She couldn't make out the words, but she didn't need to. She'd heard enough of these conversations before.

Oh, her parents were good at missing all the ways she'd changed over the years since the accident. She was good at hiding her life from them. But there were always minor things they disapproved of, especially Daddy. A pair of tight jeans became a conversation; a missed curfew when she forgot to come up with an excuse to spend the night at Rusty's was a problem—to say nothing of her daddy's reaction every time he saw her red leather boots.

Tonight was the worst thing he'd ever caught her doing, but it was far from the worst thing she'd ever done. Even so, she wouldn't get punished for it. Not formally. Reverend Shaw Moore never sent her to her room or took away her privileges. He simply judged her. With his eyes. With his words. With the way he held back any overt expression of his love.

Chapter 11

It was Ren's first time in a courtroom, but not nearly his first experience with a legal proceeding. He'd filled out plenty of legal forms, from insurance documents to vehicle registrations to whatever his mom needed him to do on her behalf on the bad days. That included going over the divorce papers once his dad finally got around to signing them years after they'd first been sent out.

Ren even filled out the emancipation paperwork that would have allowed him to legally live on his own, but his mom convinced him not to follow through with it. She'd been the one who insisted he come to Bomont, that he live with his uncle.

Yeah. That worked out well. On his very first day here he got a traffic summons. Then again, this courtroom was by far the most relaxed legal situation he'd ever been in.

The judge was having a tough time concentrating on

the business before him, like he couldn't wait to get out of his black robes and head to the fishing hole or something. It didn't much matter, though; Officer Herb more than made up for the judge's apparent disinterest.

Word had spread through town about the party at the drive-in. Rumor was Officer Herb had gotten an earful from the council over the weekend, seeing as how he'd only just left before the wild, impure dancing broke out. The drive-in hadn't been fined, since no one in law enforcement had actually been a witness to the festivities. Even Reverend Shaw had only seen two dancers. That much was clear when Ren got a glare from the reverend during Sunday services. Uncle Wes didn't bother stopping them on the way out afterward to chat with the reverend and his wife.

Ariel had been at church, too, but she didn't say anything to Ren. The whole congregation knew that she'd been dancing with him, but her father must have left that part out when he told the rest of the council about the party. It was the worst-kept secret in town, but everyone silently agreed to let the reverend deal with it himself.

Ren tried to put all that out of his mind and focus on the judge in the small Bomont County courtroom. He had just made his formal request to either reschedule or avoid his punishment altogether; all he needed now was the ruling.

"And why do you think you're above serving your

penalty in Saturday school, Mr. McCormack?" the judge asked.

Ren was prepared for the attitude. It was all that he seemed to get in this town. Giving it back to a judge would only cause more trouble. "I don't think I'm above any-one—"

Wes leaned in between them to address the judge directly. "Hey, Joey, he's got a job over at Andy's cotton mill."

Judge Joey leaned forward in a whisper. "Wes, call me Judge, would ya?" He motioned to the baseball cap Wes was wearing. "And . . . ?"

Wes took off the cap. He'd told Ren earlier that he knew the judge, but Ren wasn't sure what that meant in this small town. His uncle also knew the councilman/principal, but that didn't stop the guy from giving him grief about a neon sign that he still hadn't taken down.

"Okay, Judge Joey," Wes said, holding his cap in his hands. "Could you show some mercy here? He was play-ing his music too loud. Just about as loud as you used to play Grand Funk in that old Impala you and me used to roll in. Remember that, Judge?"

The judge paused to consider this. "You'll get Andy to verify his employment?"

Officer Herb tried to jump in to protest, but Wes cut him off.

"Yes, Judge, I will. Can I get back to the car lot now?"

Judge Joey slammed his gavel to end the proceedings. "Sentence suspended."

Ren wanted to ask if that was the end of it. It seemed like it was. Considering this crazy town, he never expected to get off so lightly, but he knew when to keep his mouth shut.

"We're at your house this Saturday?" Joey asked. The "judge" part of him dropped the moment his gavel banged on the desk.

"Kickoff's at two," Wes said. "Go Dawgs!"

"Sic 'em!" Judge Joey barked out as they left.

Officer Herb was pissed. It probably had more to do with the grief he was getting about the party at the drive-in. Maybe he heard that Ren was the one dancing when the reverend came in. Only been in town for a month, and he was flouting the laws again. Ren would have to keep an eye out for Herb. He was sure the officer would be watching him.

Ren was still basking in the victory as they left the courthouse. "Thanks for that, Uncle Wes," Ren said. "I figured I'd at least get some kind of community service or something."

"You're lucky. Not everyone's got this town on lock-down like I do." Wes practically beamed with pride. Ren did appreciate the help, but he didn't yet feel indebted to his uncle, even with all Wes had done for him in the past month. It didn't make up for the years before that.

"Since you and the judge are so chummy, maybe you

108

could have him explain this whole ban on dancing thing to me," Ren said as they waited for the traffic light to turn green so they could cross to Wes's truck. "I mean, whatever happened to the separation of church and state?"

"What does the church have to do with it?"

"It seems to have everything to do with everything around here." The light changed and they started to cross. "Let me ask you a question: if there's a football game on Sunday and you want to buy a beer, can you?"

"You can't buy beer on Sundays," Wes said, as if the mere idea was ludicrous.

"Why not?"

"Because of church."

"You can up in Boston," Ren pointed out as they got into the truck. "Why not in Bomont?"

Wes paused before he started the truck. "It's simple: Sunday is God's day. If you want to drink beer on God's day, you need to buy it on beer's day. And that's Saturday. It's right there in the Bible, if you don't believe me. The separation of God and beer." Wes cracked a smile that was supposed to let Ren know he thought the rules were silly, too, but there wasn't anything they could do about them. "And if God said it, I believe it. That settles it."

Wes turned the ignition, putting an end to the conversation. Uncle Wes talked about nothing important as they made the short ride back to the car lot. Ren's VW waited there for him. He had to get to the cotton mill—didn't want to be any later for his job than he already was.

He'd let Andy know he might run a bit behind after school because of the court date. Andy had been pretty cool about it; he thought the law was boneheaded, too. Ren knew he had a good thing with this boss and didn't want to mess around, even though he could have probably stopped for a snack before heading to work.

The VW Bug made the long trip out to the mill in good time. After a quick change of clothes, Ren got to work moving some heavy bags of mulch and stacking them onto a pallet for storage. Andy had decided to start Ren out with the less mechanical work before training him on the machines. Ren had already heard too many horror stories about missing fingers and whatnot, so he wasn't in a big rush to learn the inner workings of the heavy machinery.

He was sweaty and smelling of mulch when he got the surprise of his life: Ariel was standing in the doorway. She was about as far from covered in grime as you could get. It didn't seem like she'd faired all that badly in the punishment department, seeing as how she wasn't home locked in her room right now. Ren kind of wished her folks had been rougher on her, if only to save him from the awkwardness of having her see him like this.

She was all business, standing in the doorway without so much as a smile on her face. "Chuck Cranston wants to see you at his daddy's racetrack tomorrow at two o'clock."

Ren had about a dozen responses to that one, but he

went with the most direct. "Oh yeah? What happens at two?"

"Show up and you'll find out."

He moved toward her, still keeping a bit of distance to avoid sharing his scent. "How come he sent you to tell me?"

Now she cracked a smile. "I volunteered."

She turned on her heel and left before Ren could say anything more. He wasn't sure what he would've said to her as he watched her move off. It was obvious that she was messing with him, but how did she mean it? Did she volunteer because she wanted to see him, or because she wanted to make Chuck jealous? It was probably a combination of the two.

Ren was okay with that.

Chapter 12

Ren had only been in Bomont for a month, and already he had an entourage. Well, "posse" might be a better word. It felt good to have Willard, Woody, Etta, and Rusty beside him as he went out to the center of the dirt track at Cranston Speedway. Walking into something like this alone was just asking for trouble.

He was surprised when Rusty met up with them earlier instead of going with Ariel. It was like she'd made herself part of their group even though her best friend played for the other team.

The way that Rusty and Willard were getting closer was hard to miss—for everyone but them. Willard played dumb anytime Ren mentioned her, acting like he had no clue what Ren was talking about. But the shy smile that always crossed Willard's face was a dead giveaway. As they walked across the track, Ren couldn't help but notice that Willard was keeping himself in front of her, as if Chuck and his buddies were about to leap out and attack or something.

"If that hog tries anything, I'm gonna pound him," Willard said to Ren through clenched teeth.

"Willard, no fighting," Rusty warned.

"No promises," Willard replied.

Smiling right now would ruin the tense mood, but Ren thought it was kind of cute how Willard and Rusty already acted like an old married couple.

Chuck leaned back on top of an old tractor in the middle of the field, smoking something that wasn't legal in Bomont or Boston. His three followers from school were at the foot of the tractor, along with Ariel. Why Chuck, who obviously had graduated a few years ago, hung out with high school kids didn't make much sense to Ren. Probably no one Chuck's own age would put up with him.

That wasn't entirely true. A woman who looked a couple years older than Chuck was with them as well. No telling what her story was. "The high school field trip is here," the woman said. As if she had any right to judge them, considering she was hanging with their classmates.

Chuck hopped into the tractor seat and powered up the machine. "Hey, city mouse! Dance with this!"

The posse scattered as Chuck rolled the tractor straight for them. Everyone moved but Ren. He wasn't going to let some idiot scare him off as soon as he got there. The guy may be an ass, but he wouldn't kill anyone. Not intentionally, anyway. But there was always the chance that he'd lose control of the tractor and run over Ren. Chuck did seem the type who could accidentally kill someone.

Ren worried that might happen here as the tractor inched closer to him. He started to rethink his stand.

At the last second, Chuck pulled off to the right. Ren felt the wind off the tractor as it made the sudden move and dumped a bucketful of dirt in front of four beat-up school buses.

People with way too much time on their hands had painted the buses in crazy graffiti. Three of the buses were dark and menacing, with flames and skulls and all kinds of things meant to intimidate. The fourth bus was orange and yellow, with rows of stuffed animals strapped to the sides and front like it was meant for some kiddie party. There wasn't much doubt who that bus was meant for. Chuck shut down the tractor and climbed off it. He didn't bother with pleasantries. "We race these buses in a figure eight. Like this." He drew a figure eight in the dirt with the tip of his shoe, as if Ren needed to see it to understand. "In a figure eight."

None of the old buses looked like they were in any

shape to race, especially not on the rough track. If you could even call it a track; with all the trailers out of the center, it wasn't much more than a big dirt pit.

"Two things you gotta be worried about," Chuck warned. "Your corners and your intersections." He pointed to Rich, who stood directly in the middle of the dirt pit where the figure eight came together. Rich waved back as if they couldn't see him just fine on their own.

Not for the first time, Ren wondered why he was wasting his time with Chuck and his bozos. One glance at Ariel answered the question. She was still ignoring him like usual, but this time the peeks she took were in his direction, not Chuck's. There might even have been some concern in those eyes, but Ren wasn't sure if that was just wishful thinking on his part. Either way, it wasn't something he needed to be focusing on at the moment.

"You fall behind, you're gonna get hit by the leader," Chuck said. "You pull ahead, and you might get slammed by the guy in last place. Good luck. We'll make sure you get a proper burial."

It was supposed to sound threatening, but it was more obnoxious posturing than anything else. Ren didn't remember actually agreeing to race, but he couldn't back out now. If he did that, he'd never hear the end of it from these guys. More importantly, he'd never have a shot at dancing with Ariel again.

Ren's posse gathered back around him after Chuck walked off. "Saw a race over in Camden where one of the buses burst into flames," Willard said. "Barbequed the driver like a hog on a spit."

"Right." Ren nodded. Like he needed to know that. This was insane. Couldn't they just fight, like normal people? Sure, Chuck looked like he knew his way around a weight room, but Ren's gymnastics training kept him in good condition. More than a few guys back in Boston had made the mistake of thinking that just because he could handle a pommel horse he couldn't dish out a pummeling of his own.

School bus racing? How does someone even come up with that? He looked over the four buses again. No matter how much paint they threw on them, it didn't hide the fact that each one was more rickety than the next. He knew a thing or two about cars, but these hulking beasts were way outside his comfort zone.

He didn't even bother trying to go for the flaming skull bus. Stepping straight up to the fuzzy animal bus said more about him that any attempt at posturing. It didn't matter what the bus looked like on the outside in this race—it was more about the driver behind the wheel. And this driver didn't have a clue what he was getting himself into.

It wasn't a good start when the door refused to open for him. Rather than putting his tail between his legs and asking for help, Ren threw his weight into it and forced the door open. A minor success. Hopefully not the last one of the afternoon. Willard and Woody piled in after him as Ren got accustomed to the driver's seat. He'd never seen a bus from this angle before. The seat was much higher above the road than he was used to. But that wasn't the only difference.

The dashboard was almost nonexistent. Most of the circuits were jury-rigged in some way, with wires crisscrossing in front of him. Some even hung loose, attached to nothing but air. Woody walked Ren through the basics of bus driving, like he'd been through this kind of thing before. It was all Ren could do to keep up. Once he thought he had it, Woody moved on to the more important rules.

"All right," Woody said. "If she flips over, just crawl out the side window."

"Make sure you got your seatbelt on." Willard pulled at the partially torn strap. It wasn't going to stop anything. "But if she catches fire, just keep crawling."

Woody continued as the two of them fought to get the words out. "Once you get her running fast—"

"Hammer down. Don't get loose."

"You'll want to break around corners. Pump it with your foot real hard."

"Pump it real good," Willard emphasized in an ominous tone.

"This all sounds pretty dangerous," Ren said, trying to keep the fear out of his voice. "I mean, we could get killed, right?"

Woody clapped a hand on Ren's shoulder. "What's this 'we,' white man?"

With a couple good luck wishes, Woody and Willard hurried out of the bus, leaving Ren behind. He'd been on his own a lot in his life. But he'd never felt quite so alone before, even though he could hear Rusty and Etta cheering him on from the stands before the race even started.

Theirs weren't the only voices he could hear: Chuck's obnoxious mouth carried right through the broken window beside Ren's head, along with the last of the sweet-smelling smoke from his joint.

"Okay, let's kick this pig!" Chuck shouted for Ren's benefit. "Caroline, you gonna be on the inside or the outside?"

The woman they'd never bothered to introduce said, "I'll be on the outside. Move my way up your tailpipe."

Ren watched as the woman held out a flask to Ariel. "Need a swig, Goldilocks?" Ariel shook her head. "No? Oh, that's right, little girl. You're underage." Caroline cackled with laughter, like she'd just made the funniest joke ever. *Great.* Just what Ren needed. As if the race wasn't a dumb enough idea to start with, two of the racers were either drunk or high.

I should call this off, he thought.

He checked to make sure his seatbelt was tight instead.

Chuck giggled as he stumbled up the steps into his bus.

"Whoa, baby," Ariel said. "Are you sure you're up to this? You've had a lot to smoke."

He shook her off. "Don't be telling me I've had enough."

"I didn't say you had enough. I said you had *a lot*."

"You wanna lecture somebody, go tell Sweet Buns to start his engine."

Ren never wanted to hit anyone more than he wanted to punch Chuck in the face right then. This race was all about Ariel, and the guy treated her like crap. She was just looking out for him, being the lone voice of reason when even Ren couldn't bring himself to stop this. Why didn't she see that she could do so much better?

Ren revved his engine to let them know he got the message as Chuck shut the door on Ariel. She stood fuming for a moment before climbing into the back of Chuck's truck and holding tight as Travis pulled out from between the buses.

"There's one warm-up lap before the green flag drops," Ariel shouted as they passed Ren. "You got that?"

Ren gave a thumbs up, but she was already gone.

The voice of Chuck's flunky, Rich, came blasting out of the PA. "Gentlemen," he said. "You, too, Caroline. Start your engines!"

All four buses followed Travis, who was using the truck as a pace car. Russell was on Ren's left, Chuck was on his right, and Caroline was down at the end. Ariel stood in front of them all in the truck bed, holding the yellow caution flag.

"Hey, where's the green flag?" she called up to Travis.

"Improvise!" he shouted back.

She looked down at her own tank top. It was green enough. With a grin, she removed it, revealing the pink bra underneath. Chuck and his buddies cheered and waved at her, shouting out catcalls. Ren just shook his head. He didn't turn away, but he also wasn't going to act like those asses about it. Ariel waved her shirt over her head and let out an excited *whoop* before she dropped her arm to start the race.

"Put the spurs to her, Ren!" Rusty shouted over the noise of the engines.

Ren pushed down on the gas and took off, neck and neck with Chuck. The bus rumbled beneath him as he struggled with the wheel to keep it on the straightaway. Nothing responded the way he expected. Even the brakes felt light as he went into the turn.

"Pump the brakes! Pump the brakes!" Woody yelled.

Ren stomped on the brake pedal, but the bus kept rolling on into the curve. He sideswiped an embankment. It slowed him enough that he could take back control of the behemoth, but Chuck, Russell, and Caroline pulled ahead.

Wes (Ray McKinnon) makes Ren (Kenny Wormald) a really interesting offer. If he can fix the beat-up old Bug, it will be his.

Ariel (Julianne Hough) plays the part of the demure preacher's daughter, carefully hiding her wilder side.

Ariel gets her adrenaline fix with a dangerous lap around the track.

Reverend Shaw Moore (Dennis Quaid) and his wife, Vi (Andie MacDowell), welcome Ren into their congregation.

Ren makes a memorable first impression as the new kid at school.

Woody (Ser'Darius William Blain), Willard (Miles Teller), and Ren talk cars and girls—and one girl in particular.

Ariel's look for a night out is a far cry from her Sunday best.

The bus race at Cranston Speedway comes to a fiery end.

Ren cuts loose when he thinks no one is watching.

Ariel and Ren share a quiet moment together.

Ren uses every free moment teaching Willard
some smooth moves for the dance.

Ren and Ariel kick up their heels outside town limits.

Willard shows off his new dance moves!

Ren got the bus back in gear and slipped into fourth place, coming up on Caroline. She slammed her bus into his to let Ren know she didn't like that. Metal smashed into metal, jarring him to his core. *Nobody said anything about bumper cars.*

Caroline kept on him, not letting up as they drove toward the intersection of the figure eight, with Russell heading right for them.

This is gonna be ugly, Ren thought. If only he could get away from her, he might be able to avoid the coming wreck. He tried to wave Caroline off, but she was so focused on him that she didn't see anything else. The three buses were heading for a huge crash.

Gotta do something, Ren thought. *But what?*

The brakes were still sluggish, but Ren didn't see any other option. He slammed both feet onto the pedal, jamming it all the way down to the floor. Clouds of dust kicked up behind him as the brake finally engaged and Caroline pulled ahead. She never saw Russell coming.

BAM! The collision echoed throughout the track. Russell's bus T-boned Caroline's. She flipped to the side, skidding to a stop as Russell continued on as if she'd never been there in the first place.

As he passed her, Ren saw Caroline climbing out the window, cursing Russell. She seemed okay enough to Ren. He continued on as a couple of Chuck's other unnamed buddies pushed Caroline's bus off the track with a pair of tractors.

The bus got easier to steer the longer Ren was behind the wheel, but the brakes were still hit or miss. This was too dangerous. Too stupid. He wasn't going to die just to make a point or impress some girl.

He was about to pull out of the race when Russell rear-ended him in a violent smash. Ren cursed as the brakes failed. His foot banged the pedal against the floor, but it was useless. He didn't even feel any pressure—the brakes were completely gone. He couldn't stop this now if he wanted to.

But that wasn't the worst part. He saw sparks flying out the back of the bus in the rearview mirror. He heard metal grinding against metal. Something must have broken in the undercarriage.

The sparks caught on one of the stuffed animals and quickly turned into flames. His friends screamed a mix of cheers and fear from the stands.

His wasn't the only bus damaged. Russell did more harm to his own ride with the crash, and he spun out of control and came to a hard stop. It was just Ren and Chuck now.

Ren threw all his strength into steering as he hit the corner with no brakes. It almost felt like the wheels were coming off the ground. Woody was on the edge of the track holding a fire extinguisher as the flames grew. They were inside the bus now.

"No brakes!" Ren yelled.

He barely heard Woody's "Uh-oh" as he passed.

The fire spread to the seats in back. The heat of the flames got closer, turning the metal bus into a pressure cooker. Ren slammed his foot down on the floor over and over again in a pointless attempt to engage brakes that weren't there.

Rich held up a sign that read FINAL LAP as the fiery bus passed. "Get the checkered flag ready, Ariel," he yelled. "Chuck's gonna win this one."

As if Ren gave a damn about the race anymore. He was more concerned with getting out of this alive. At this speed, with the fire behind him, even if he tried to crash into something to stop the bus, he could end up killing someone—most likely himself.

The intersection was coming up again. Ren and Chuck barreled toward it from opposite sides of the track. They were going to get there at the same time. Ren knew Chuck wasn't going to stop. Winning was on the line.

He could see Chuck through the big front window. The guy was screaming something at him. Probably telling Ren to get out of the way.

Ren's mind raced. With the brakes gone, he couldn't stop. If he tried to turn at this speed, he could flip the bus. That only left one option.

"Aw, what the hell." Ren held onto his seatbelt and stepped on the gas.

Chuck never wavered.

Ren's bus plowed into Chuck's with a crash of twisted metal that sent shockwaves reverberating through the track. Chuck's bus flipped over as it was knocked clear by Ren's speeding missile of a vehicle. Ren continued to the finish line after one more hairpin turn.

Ariel waved the checkered flag among the cheers from Ren's friends. She had a look of disappointment on her face as he blew past, but maybe a bit of a sly smile for him as well. It was hard to tell as the bus went barreling around the track, continuing on a path of destruction.

Woody and Willard ran alongside the bus. The impact from the crash had slowed it enough that they could jump in through the open door, but it wasn't enough. "It won't stop!" Ren yelled.

"Downshift! Downshift!" Willard hollered.

Ren *was* downshifting. It didn't do any good.

Woody was in the back with the fire extinguisher, fighting a losing battle.

They were heading back toward Chuck's flipped bus again. This time, Ren didn't think they'd be so lucky.

"Okay!" Willard screamed. "Off the bus! Abandon bus!"

Ren unclipped his seatbelt and they leaped from the bus as Chuck ran out of its path.

Ren rolled as he hit the ground, coming up in time to see the fiery bus plow into the dead one. The sound of the impact was deafening. An explosion blew as the gas tank caught fire. Debris rained down on the track.

And then silence as the flames devoured the vehicles.

Everyone froze, taking in the devastation.

Willard was the first to regain his senses, breaking the silence with laughter and singing, "The wipers on the bus go *Boom! Boom! Boom!*"

But Ren wasn't focused on the flames. All he saw was Ariel watching him.

For once, she didn't look away.

Chapter 13

Ren's body still ached from the race. Days later, the muscles he strained while fighting with the steering wheel and the bruises he got from tumbling out of the bus were not-so-subtle reminders of his own stupidity. For a while he worried he'd broken something important, but he seemed to be healing okay. Wes didn't even ask him where the bruises came from, but Lulu was making extra big breakfasts, as if trying to make up for the fact that he was having such a hard time fitting in around Bomont.

But Ren wasn't having as many problems as before. He had friends now. Several, in fact. Word spread quickly around school about his victory and spectacular dismount from an exploding bus. Even Ariel caught his eye more often in the halls, and not just when Rusty was around, taking pains to point him out.

He sat in the school library doing some research on a history paper when Chuck's loser friend, Rich, grabbed a seat beside him like they were friends.

"Chuck's pretty sore about losing that race," Rich said, in a voice slightly above a whisper. The librarian, Mr. Parker, lifted his head to watch them. "You really pulled that win outta nowhere, bro. Up top." He raised a hand, but Ren ignored him. The librarian squinted his eyes their way, but then went back to reading his own book.

Rich continued, undaunted. "Yeah, Bomont blows. I don't have to tell you. I been to Chicago. St. Louis. Been to some of the clubs in New York. I got people. Connections."

Ren tried very hard not to laugh. "Connections, huh?"

Rich nodded slowly and meaningfully. "Mm-hm . . ."

Ren wasn't sure what the meaning was, but he knew he didn't want any part of it. He closed his book and moved deeper into the library.

Rich didn't take the hint. He followed, digging around for something in his pocket. "Hey, man. Let me ask you something. You get high?" Rich pulled a joint out and waved it in front of Ren's face.

What was this idiot doing with a joint in the middle of the day at school? Ren already had trouble with the law. He didn't need any more. He tried to ignore Rich, but the guy had him cornered in the stacks.

"I do," Rich said. "Every day. We could burn one after

school. You and me. You know, city mouse and country mouse, getting blazed."

Ren didn't think for a second that this guy had any interest in friendship. Something else was going on. "What makes you think I'm anything like you?"

Rich slipped the joint into Ren's shirt pocket. "Look, this here is a take-homer. You need more, just holler. I'm your man."

Ren pulled the joint out, pushing it back at Rich. "Hey. I don't want this. Take it back."

Rich moved off. "Hey, it's cool. It's cool."

"No. It's not cool. Take it back."

"Hey!" Mr. Parker stood at the end of the stacks, not ten feet away.

This was not good. Not good at all. Ren froze with the joint in his hand while Rich took off down another aisle, leaving him with the contraband.

Mr. Parker moved toward Ren. "What is that?"

Ren palmed the joint. "What's what?"

"In your hand. Let me see."

If Ren opened his hand he was dead. In school. In Bomont.

Possession wasn't something Judge Joey could just gloss over, no matter how many ball games Uncle Wes invited him to.

Uncle Wes. He wasn't going to like this at all. He'd never believe Ren now. There was no way he could let the librarian see the joint. Ren saw an escape route and took it, heading for the bathroom across the way.

The librarian followed. "Stop, I said."

But Ren didn't stop. Not until he was in a stall and the joint was swirling down the toilet, the evidence securely flushed. By the time Mr. Parker stumbled in after him, the water was clear.

Ren tried to push past the librarian, but Mr. Parker wasn't having it. He marched Ren straight down the hall and into the principal's office. Before he even knew it, calls were made, and his good buddy Officer Herb was on the case.

"I don't know if you appreciate the seriousness of this offense, Mr. McCormack," Officer Herb said. "Drug possession on campus can not only get you expelled, you could serve time. Real time. You got me?"

Ren did get it. He got it better than the adults in the room probably did. They just saw him as trouble. Like it or hate it, Bomont was the only home he had right now. Ren couldn't risk bringing his uncle to another court date.

"We don't tolerate it, Ren," Principal Dunbar said. "Not in this school. What do you have to say for your-self?"

When he saw Russell and Travis outside the window enjoying his situation, his fear turned to anger. He used that emotion to mount his defense. "For three years I competed in gymnastics. We had random drug screening. If I ever smoked weed, I'd be kicked off the team."

"I saw the joint in his hand," Mr. Parker sputtered. "I saw it."

Ren bit back. "So, you know what one looks like, huh?"

The librarian was flustered. "Well . . . I . . ."

"Were you going to smoke it or were you gonna sell it?" Officer Herb pressed on with the interrogation. "Which is it?"

They didn't even *want* to listen. He was guilty until proven innocent. And even then they'd still be out for him. Ren shook his head. "Oh my God."

"Mr. Parker here said you were hanging with Rich Sawyer when this went down," the principal said.

"I barely know that prick."

"Hey," Officer Herb said. "Language."

Principal Dunbar—*Roger*—leaned forward with concern in his eyes. Obviously, he was playing the good cop, since there clearly wasn't one in the room. "Ren, level with me. Was it Rich's joint? You can tell me."

Three faces stared at Ren while he decided how to respond. He didn't care about protecting Rich; that was a no-brainer. Getting a reputation as a snitch wasn't a concern, either. Most people he knew would've told him to hang the jerk out to dry without a second thought. No, this was about choosing sides. The people in this town lived in fear of the stupid laws, the authority that put the rules ahead of living. If he gave in here, it would be the first of many defeats to come.

Ren met each of their eyes, one by one, as he spoke calmly and firmly. "I don't do drugs. Test me if you want." He pointed at Mr. Parker. "But if it comes out clean, I want this guy investigated for barging into the bathroom stall with me."

It felt as if a chilled breeze had blown through the room. The librarian was horrified; Officer Herb was angry. But the principal took it all in, wheels turning in his mind. He was the one who worried Ren the most. He'd used every weapon in his arsenal; if he still got in trouble, it wasn't for lack of trying. "That's got to be a violation on a few levels," he added, to push the point. "You know what I'm saying?"

"All right, Ren," Roger said. "Since we don't have the evidence, I'm going to let you off with a warning."

Officer Herb shook his head. This was the second time Ren had gotten one over on him.

"But you need to understand that life is not some big party," the principal continued. "I don't care what rap music says—marijuana is wrong. You want to go looking for cheap thrills, do it outside of my school. Do it outside Bomont. Understand?"

Ren sighed. Even if he had turned Rich in, they would still have believed he was just as much of a problem. There was no winning with these people.

"You know," Roger said. "I knew your mother. I knew

Sandy. And she had a wild streak in her, too. Running off up north to live the high life might have been fun, but it also led to her getting into some unexpected trouble."

Anger brewed under the surface. Ren did all that he could to hold it in. The principal was trying to rile him. He couldn't let the man see that it was working. "Unexpected trouble? I'm thinking when you say 'unexpected trouble,' you mean me. Right?" He clutched the arm of the chair. They'd made their decision about him before he ever arrived in town. "Believe me. Don't believe me. Suspend me. Put me in jail. Whatever." Ren stood suddenly. The move came so quickly that Officer Herb's hand reflexively dropped to his sidearm. "But do me a favor, would you?" Ren continued. "Keep my mother's name outta your mouth."

He burst out of the office without waiting to be dismissed. Officer Herb called after him, but the principal said to let him go.

Ren *wanted* to go. Out of the school. Out of this backwoods town. Out of everything. But he could only do one of those things, so he headed for the parking lot.

How dare they? How dare *they?* To say his mom led the high life. Yeah, he'd show them the high life. Nothing higher than the meds she was on to control the pain. So fancy the life they led, with both of them working two jobs to scrape by and him still managing to go to school and get decent grades. It was a wild time.

Wild.

He was so mad that for the first time since he got there, he completely failed to notice Ariel in the empty hall. He blew right past her. But she certainly noticed him, and hurried to follow, trying to get *his* attention for once.

"Hey, McCormack. What's your rush?"

Ren didn't answer. He was too angry to speak, and tired of the games. And he was too afraid of what he might say. Vi said she knew his mom, too. What would she have told her daughter about Sandy? What was everyone around this town saying about her? Saying about him?

"What?" Ariel asked as they reached his car. Her tone was light. She had no idea what kind of mood he was in. "You trying to ignore me?"

He jumped into the car, slamming the door shut between them. "I'm doing the best I can."

Ariel froze in her tracks. She wasn't used to getting that kind of reaction from guys. Ren was taking his anger out on the wrong person, but he didn't care. If everyone in this town stopped giving him a hard time, maybe they'd all see that he wasn't the person they thought he was.

He fired up the engine and blared his rap music, daring Officer Herb to come out and write him up again. He didn't stick around for it to happen. Ren peeled out of the parking lot, leaving Ariel and the whole damn school in his rearview mirror.

Times like this, Ren wished the VW Bug could really bring up some speed. He needed to put some distance between himself and Bomont. But where would he go? He didn't even know which road to take to get to Atlanta. And then what? Spend the night wandering aimlessly around the city?

Ren didn't need to wander. He needed to focus. To work out his aggression.

He needed to move.

Ren swung a hard right at the next intersection. He knew just the place to go: the old abandoned scrap yard. It was far enough outside of town that nobody would be there to bother him.

His iPod shuffled from the rap song to an old punk tune. Just the music he needed for the drive. He screamed along with the singer, venting his frustration.

The scrap yard was as deserted as he remembered it. *Good*. He didn't have to slow the car as he weaved between the mounds of scrap, leaving plumes of dust in his wake. He headed straight for the open loading dock.

The tires screeched on the concrete floor as he tore through the warehouse, dodging rusty car parts. He finally came to a stop deep inside the building, where he was truly alone.

He pulled the iPod along with him as he got out of the car. As frantic as he felt, he was careful not to cut the wire that kept it attached to the speakers. He wanted the music, and he needed it to be loud.

It had to be something he could move to. Something

that matched the mood he was in. Shaking the iPod, he switched songs. A generic hip-hop tune blared from the speakers.

"No."

Another shake brought up a rock song. Better, but not enough.

"Uh-uh."

He shook the iPod again. *Nothing.* And again. *Nothing.* He shook it so hard that only random beeps came out of the speakers.

"Shit!" Ren threw the iPod against the hood of the car. It finally settled on the perfect song. A blend of alternative rock with a heavy beat and wild guitar riffs. Perfect for the mood he was in. He kicked the garbage and rusted cabinets around him along with the beat.

"Talk about my mother!" he yelled to no one. "You better keep my mother's name out of your mouth, you righteous bitch. You don't know! You don't know shit!"

Emotion overwhelmed Ren, the emotions he'd been holding in since the funeral, since he got to this damn town. Tears welled in his eyes. He covered his face with his arms, trying to hold it all back. His hands balled into fists as the sadness turned to rage.

A huge barrel got in his way and he knocked it over, sending the rats inside scurrying. "Get out of here!" he yelled at them. "Go on, you rat freakin' piece of—"

He picked up the barrel and threw it at the rats. It

landed with a bang, followed by another bang as he flung a metal pipe that smashed through a window. It felt good. It felt even better with the next pipe. And the next.

Out of pipes, Ren paused to catch his breath. The song shifted into a guitar solo and Ren lost himself in the music. His body began to move.

Fueled by his anger, Ren took off like a rocket, moving to the music, leaping and twirling. Part dance, part gymnastics, his movements were violent, sweaty, raw.

He climbed up to the rafters among the metal beams and chains that went in all directions. Leaping up onto a pipe, he spun around on it like a horizontal bar. Over and around he swung, rubbing his hands raw, until he let go, flipping in the air.

He stuck his landing on a dusty old crate that smashed into pieces beneath him. Lost in the rage, he kicked away the debris.

The wild dance took him all around the warehouse. Cutting a hand on some glass didn't stop him. The heat from his movements didn't slow him down. He flung off his sweaty shirt and kept moving. Blood dripped from the cut on his hand and sweat dripped from his body, drenching his undershirt.

Covered in dust, he went old-school with break dancing, spinning on the ground until the frustration left his body and he collapsed, utterly exhausted and drained of emotion. He'd danced through most of his anger, but his body was still filled with energy. He jumped when Ariel stepped out of the shadows.

"What are you doing here? Did you follow me? I thought I was alone."

"Not in this town, you're not. There's eyes everywhere." Her voice softened. "So what was all that?"

"All what?"

She mimicked some of his dance moves. "All that stuff."

"Just letting off some steam," Ren said. He felt naked in front of her. Exposed. How long was she watching him? "I'm sure you got your own wicked ways."

"What's that supposed to mean? You think I'm a slut or something?"

Ren laughed to break the tension. She was ready to fight. "I think you been kissed a lot." He picked his shirt up off the dirty floor and put it on. "Where's Lugnut?"

"You mean Chuck?" she asked, as if she didn't know exactly who he was talking about. "He doesn't own me. He acts like he does, but he doesn't." She moved closer. "You think I'm small town, huh?"

He leaned in. "I think Bomont is a small town."

Their bodies hung there, inches from one another. It was a different game of chicken than the one Ren had played with her boyfriend.

Ariel was the first to blink. "You wanna see something?"

Yes, he most certainly did.

Chapter 14

Ren drove behind Rusty's car as they headed out of the scrap yard and made a left onto the rural highway. He had to wonder how Ariel had time to get the car and still follow him. Probably had her own set of keys. It seemed like the kind of thing Rusty would do for her friend. It wasn't fair to think Ariel took advantage of people all the time. Jumping to conclusions, the way everyone did with him. Ren didn't really know her well, but he thought he might understand her. She wasn't the tough girl that she pretended to be. He could see the truth in her eyes: the brief flash of fear when her father showed up at the drive-in. The few glances Ren caught when she was ignoring him, as if she didn't want him to talk to her, but she didn't want him to stop trying, either.

He pulled in behind her when she stopped off the side of the road in a clearing. Nothing but trees around as the sun started setting on the late autumn afternoon. For a brief moment, Ren wondered if this was some kind of a trick—that Ariel was leading him into a trap where he was about to get jumped by Chuck and his friends. But it was an easy thought to dismiss. Ariel wouldn't do that; now that she was finally looking at him, he could see that in her eyes, too.

But it didn't explain why she'd led him through the trees all the way out to an abandoned rail yard. All the decaying old railcars gave the place the feeling that it was haunted. Little bits of Bomont, discarded and forgotten.

But Ren wasn't thinking about the past as the sky went deep purple with sunset. He focused on Ariel and the soft hand she held out to help him into an empty railcar. The place was cool and dark. Ren worried about what she had in mind. Not because he wasn't ready, but because he wasn't sure *they* were. He didn't want to just go for a tumble with Ariel, to use her and be used by her. He wanted to know her first. Find out what made her so different from everyone else in this town. Then maybe some tumbling would be fun. He was a gymnast, after all.

A propane lantern sat on top of an old wooden cable spool. Ren wondered if they were crashing somebody's home as Ariel lit the lamp. Ren was awestruck as the lamplight revealed the boxcar's secret: a mural of graffiti art, song lyrics, old photos, and poetry covered the walls.

The photos showed different people in a bunch of different clothing styles, obviously from different times. Handwritten messages were everywhere. Some of the graffiti was beautiful; some was just scratched-out names and symbols. This was not the work of one person, or even a dozen.

"Everybody calls it the yearbook," Ariel explained. "I don't know when it started. Maybe about ten years ago."

A piece of writing caught Ren's attention. "What is all this?"

"Some are songs. Lyrics. Quotes from books. Stuff we're not supposed to read." She pointed to another spot on the wall. "There's some old folk songs and blues lyrics here."

Together, they read the words to some kind of odd cheer about feeling fine and cherry wine while laughing at the absurdity of the chant that was littered with "oh yeahs." And then suddenly their faces were inches away from one another. Her perfume was all he could smell, her eyes all he could see.

"You want to kiss me?" she said.

Ren was cool. "Someday."

She didn't like that. "What's this 'someday' shit? Look, I don't know what kind of city girls you've had experience with, but let me assure you, I can keep up."

He wasn't about to play her games. "You know, you got everybody else in this town fooled but me." His response startled her. "Yeah, you get wild and rowdy.

Hanging out at the dirt track, thinkin' you're hard-core. But you're just scared. I see it, because I know."

He'd found out who those five kids in the memorial were; he knew one of them had been her brother. Wes told him about it; it explained why the reverend felt the way he did. It also explained some of the connection Ren shared with her. "I know what it's like to lose somebody you love. I know what it's like to feel alone. And pissed off."

Ariel's expression softened. She was actually listening to him.

"So, yeah," he continued. "You and me could tumble right here in this railcar. But that sweat's gonna dry, and you're still gonna feel like dirt. That's Chuck's job to do. Not mine."

He'd struck a chord. That much was clear in the mix of emotions on Ariel's face. The mask had slipped, but she was quick to replace it. "Well, don't get all heavy on me."

She was deflecting, but Ren could still feel the emotions underneath. He could see her in a way that most people probably didn't. It was wonderful and terrifying at the same time. A train whistle off in the distance was the only sound between them.

Ariel broke the spell. "Hey, did you hear that?" She hopped out of the railcar. The rumbling of the train got louder as it approached. "Come on! Hurry!"

Ren followed her through the winding maze of cars, wondering what all the excitement was about. It was probably the same train that cut through Bomont a few times a day. "Wait up! Where you going?"

He lost her around one of the corners, and doubled back in the direction she must have gone. Another corner and he found her again, standing beside the train track.

"Sometimes after football games, we'd all come out here," she said with newfound energy. "Just a few of us. And when the train came we'd go at it like crazy." She smiled. "But most of the time, we'd just stand here and scream."

Ariel moved onto the tracks, standing between the rails, directly in the path of the oncoming train.

"Hey, stop fooling around," Ren said. The train was getting closer.

Ariel ignored him, throwing back her head and letting out a Heaven-splitting scream. The sound was almost drowned out by the deafening noise of the train horn.

She wasn't getting out of the way.

The train got closer. And closer.

Ren dove for her, pulling her off the tracks. They landed hard on the gravel on the other side of the train moments before it rumbled by. The horn belched curses at them, as the engineer must have seen what had almost happened.

Ariel was on her back, laughing. Ren stood up and reached a hand out to her. "Let me take you home."

. . . . .

Ariel slipped quietly into her dark house, carefully closing the front door behind her. It was the least late for curfew she'd been in a long time. It was also the one time she was actually afraid of getting caught. Funny, because she didn't really do anything that would get her in trouble tonight, certainly not compared to the things she did on other nights. It was almost expected that Daddy was waiting at the top of the stairs for her.

"It's hard to impose a curfew on the young people of my congregation when I can't even enforce it in my own home," he said, looking down on her in every way.

Ariel didn't say anything. There was nothing she could say that wouldn't start a fight. She kept her head down, focused on the stairs.

"Have you been drinking?" he asked.

"No."

"Have you been smoking anything?"

She finally looked up at him to see the familiar disappointment in his eyes. "I wasn't smoking, drinking, dancing, or reading any books I'm not supposed to. I'm just late."

"Who dropped you off just now?"

Ren's name was out of her mouth before she realized her mistake. Just because she hadn't done anything worth lying about didn't mean that honesty was the best policy.

"I don't want you to see him again," her father said.

"Why?"

"Because I've heard he's trouble."

"Trouble?" She let out a small laugh. Ren was the least trouble she'd ever been with. "Well, Daddy, man born of woman is of few days and full of trouble. Job 14:1. You know, from the Bible?"

Ariel pushed past her father, but he grabbed her arm before she could end the conversation. "Your behavior lately has been downright atrocious. And it seems to have started just as Ren McCormack arrived in town."

She just looked at him. He was so clueless about what the past few years of her life were like. "Ren's the least of your worries," she said. "Sometimes trouble's right under your nose."

She broke free and went to her room, shutting her door, closing him out. The reverend refrained from going after her.

Chapter 15

"Come here a sec, Ren."

That didn't sound good. Uncle Wes's voice was in parent mode. It wasn't a tone Ren had heard much in his life, but he knew it well enough to understand that something was up. Ren figured he knew what it was.

"Willard's waiting for me," Ren said as he stepped into the living room.

Uncle Wes was in his armchair with a beer in his hand. He motioned for Ren to sit on the couch. Wes had come home from work early. He'd been there for almost an hour now, probably waiting for Aunt Lulu and the girls to go out running errands before having this talk.

Ren sat down and braced for the worst.

"Reverend Moore came to see me at the lot today."

"Did he?" Ren said. Yep. It was exactly what he thought.

This was ridiculous. They were only a half-hour late for curfew. That was nothing. Certainly not enough to require a face-to-face meeting to discuss the situation.

"Yeah," Wes said. "Are you pursuing his daughter? Ariel?"

"Pursuing?" Ren asked.

Wes nodded. "You know what I mean. Are you interested in the reverend's daughter?"

Only a few sentences in, and Ren already hated this conversation. "What if I am?"

Wes leaned back in his chair. "If you are, you could be asking for a world of trouble."

"Look, Wes, I don't think—"

"No, Ren, *you* look. I know this move ain't been easy on you. I know you miss your mother. I miss her, too. But things are different here."

"Yeah. People keep telling me that."

"You go after the reverend's daughter, and you open yourself up to even more gossip and prying eyes. Shaw brought up the thing at school with the drugs."

Ren was glad he told his uncle about the joint in the library that morning. He wasn't about to repeat the mistake with the ticket. "I told you—"

"I know you better than that," Wes said. "Look, I wasn't there when you needed me. I get that it wasn't easy taking care of your mom, keeping the house clean and cooking the meals while you went to school. Going to your job *and* dealing with her doctors. Getting that special driver's license at thirteen so you could take your mom to dialysis. You had to grow up fast because your father was a deadbeat and your uncle was too far away to help. I probably still could have done more than I did."

This was the last thing Ren expected. "Uncle Wes—"

"Now, just let me get this out, Ren," he said. There was a tear in his uncle's eye. It made Ren uncomfortable. "I should've been there for you. And I got to live with that. But you gotta live with it, too. Just because you were forced to be an adult up in Boston doesn't mean people are going to see you the same way down here in Bomont. They just gonna think you're too big for your britches. They already do."

"Are you saying I can't go out with Ariel?"

"I'm saying nothing of the kind," Wes assured him. "I just want you to be careful. More careful than you've been. This town will give you enough grief on its own. You don't need to go inviting more of it."

Ren relaxed a bit. None of this solved his problems, but it was nice to hear. "So, what did you tell the reverend?"

"Just what I told you," Wes said. "Though I may have added something about his daughter being a bit of a troublemaker herself."

Ren wished he hadn't said that last part. It wouldn't make things easier for him and Ariel. But still, it was nice to know his uncle had his back. "Thanks, Wes."

"No need to thank me," Wes said. "That's what family does. Now, go get your friend. It ain't nice to keep people waiting." He took a swig of his beer, grabbed the remote, and turned on ESPN, effectively ending the conversation.

Ren stayed on the couch and watched his uncle for a moment. The teary eyes were gone. His full attention was on the TV, as if their talk didn't just happen. That was fine with Ren. Better that way, really. No reason to dwell on it.

. . . . .

By the time Ren picked up Willard and filled him in on what happened, Ren had worked up his anger again. It only got worse as they took the VW to the do-it-yourself car wash. He scrubbed the car so hard he worried he'd punch right through the metal.

Ren threw the rag down into a puddle of soapy water. "I don't believe this town. I bring Ariel home past her curfew last night, the next morning Reverend Moore is all up in my uncle's grille. Making threats."

"He made a threat?" Willard asked.

"He made his point," Ren said.

"You know what it is?" Willard said. "You got an attitude problem."

"*I* got an attitude problem?" Ren was astonished.

Willard nodded. "Every chance you get, you bad-mouth this town. I know we're small time, but we got satellites and cell phones just like everybody else. We've seen some progress."

Ren was having none of it—but he decided to let it pass. Willard wasn't to blame for his trouble. "Don't talk to me about progress," Ren said. "I've been here two months and I haven't seen one wet T-shirt contest."

"I know," Willard said, playing along. "What's up with that?"

"I'm sure there's a law against it. Maybe we could find a loophole." Yeah, Reverend Moore would love that.

"If you got a petition, you got my signature," Willard said, laughing.

But Ren suddenly had a thought. "You know, that's not a bad idea. We could challenge the law."

"Huh?" Willard dropped his sponge. His mind was probably filled with women in wet T-shirts. But that's not what Ren meant.

"A *dance*," he said. "Organize our own dance. I'm not talking about some drunken kegger or free-for-all orgy—"

"Why not?" Willard asked. He wasn't taking this seriously at all.

But Ren was. He was deadly serious. "No," he said. "I'm talking about a respectful, formal dance. One that's not held in a church."

"You could have it at the Bomont lockup," Willard said. "'Cuz you gotta remember, what you're talking about is against the law."

Ren's mind was already past that problem. Judge Joey and Officer Herb had already proven that the law in this town might be strict, but it wasn't final. "Let me tell you something about laws. They're meant to be challenged. Nothing's set in stone."

"The Ten Commandments were," Willard pointed out. "What's your smart aleck reply on that?" He was laughing, proud of himself for coming up with that one. Almost begging Ren to put him in his place.

Ren turned the hose on Willard, spraying him with cold water as he shouted, "Let my people go!"

Willard threw up his hands to block the water. "Quit it! Quit it! Stop!" But Ren wouldn't stop, so Willard just gave in and let the water run down his body. "All right, you wanted a wet T-shirt contest? Have at it!" Willard did a little dance as Ren hosed him down.

They finished up with the car, then drove it around town to dry it off, talking through Ren's dance idea. He didn't have the first clue how to go about getting a law overturned.

When he got home later, he thought about asking Wes and Lulu, but it was too early to bring them in on something like this. He wanted to get all his ducks in a row before creating any trouble for Wes so soon after his run-in with the reverend. This was something Ren had to do on his own for now.

He started the next day in his free period, heading back to the library. He walked up to the librarian's desk with the swagger of a man on a mission. It was all about asking the right questions.

"Can I help you with something?" Mr. Parker said. He was already on guard.

Ren's eyes scanned the library stacks, as if he were trying to figure something out. "I don't know if this would be in self-help or how-to, but I'm looking for books that can help me build my own meth lab."

He cracked a smile when Mr. Parker's eyes bugged out.

"I'm just messing with you," Ren smiled at him. "You wouldn't happen to have city records down here—like, local ordinances?"

The librarian's eyes squinted with suspicion. "What do you want with those?"

A direct answer had been the last thing Ren expected, so this came as no surprise. "I want to read them. Isn't that what you do in libraries, other than get high?"

Ren knew he was pushing it, but he wanted to keep the librarian off balance. Didn't need him asking too many questions. The plan must have worked, because Mr. Parker pointed him to the right books and left him alone to do his research, although he kept an eye on him. Ren started with the city ordinance books at the top of the stack. He wasn't sure what, exactly, he was looking for, but he began with what he knew. The accident that killed Ariel's brother and the other kids happened three years ago. All the laws came into effect after that. It was best to start with the wording of the laws, then go back and see how the other ones were changed.

The legalese in the book wasn't half as bad as some of the stuff he'd had to go through for his mom when she was at her sickest. The language of the law was pretty straightforward and direct. There were several routes he already thought he could pursue.

Once he'd thoroughly examined the law, he moved on to researching the procedures for overturning it. This was also easy enough to understand, but it didn't answer all his questions. Suddenly, he felt like the librarian's eyes weren't the only ones on him. There was a closer presence. Two, in fact.

"Look at the little bookworm," Rusty said lightly. She and Ariel were standing over him. He'd been so wrapped up in the books that he didn't even notice them. It was the first chance he'd had to talk to Ariel since he dropped her off the other night.

"Don't get him mad," she said. "He'll start dancing."

He let the comment slide. "Did you get in trouble?"

Ariel shrugged. "I heard my dad went down to your uncle's car lot. Sorry about that."

"What are you doing?" Rusty asked, pushing in on Ren, trying to see what he was reading.

He shut the book. He wasn't ready to let anyone else in on the plan. "It's top secret."

"C'mon," Ariel said in a playful tone. "You can tell us."

"Did you find that National Geographic book with all the topless tribal women?" Rusty asked. "That floated around the school for decades. My dad can describe it in frightening detail."

Ariel slipped in to read the spine of the book while Rusty distracted Ren. "*Civil Ordinances of Bomont.*"

With the cat partially out of the bag, Ren opened the book. He didn't need to tell them exactly what he was up to, but it wouldn't hurt to get their opinion on something. "There's a procedure when you want to challenge an ordinance, but it requires a petition and a public forum. That's just to get a vote." He flipped through the pages, looking for the information he needed. "Zoning restrictions . . . Spousal rights . . ."

"Wait a sec." Rusty leaned over him now. "Are you trying to overturn the ban on public dancing?" Willard must have given her a hint. It was too big a leap to make without information.

"No, he's not," Ariel said with certainty, until she saw the expression on Ren's face. "You're not, right?"

He grabbed one of the books he'd gone through earlier. "I've counted at least five ordinances that have been overturned in the past ten years. Why can't we do the same?"

"You know if you challenge the ordinance, you'd be going up against my father," Ariel said. Ren couldn't tell if she thought that was a good or a bad thing. Maybe she didn't know, either.

"I'd be challenging the law. There's a difference." Ren

caught the meaningful look the two girls shared. Maybe Willard was right; Ren could come off like he was against the town. He certainly would have his reasons, but if he was going to get support for this measure, he needed allies.

"I'm not just trying to stick it to this town," he said. "I can understand all these other rules, up to a point. But dancing in public? It's bullsh—" Mr. Parker's eyes were on all three of them. Ren lowered his voice. "It's wrong."

Rusty took a seat beside him with newfound excitement. "Well, I think if you're serious about this, there's one thing we have to do. And it's crucial."

"What's that?" Ariel asked, joining in.

Rusty's grin lit up the library. "Research."

Chapter 16

It was a tight squeeze, fitting four bodies into the VW Bug for the long ride out of town. And that was even without the oversize cowboy hat on Willard's head.

They survived the jam-packed ride to their mystery destination. All Ariel and Rusty had said was that they should wear their dancing shoes. The neon cowboy boots above the entrance to the country music club provided the remaining answers.

Ren was never a big fan of country music, but just seeing the bar full of people kicking up their heels in an energetic line dance was enough to convert him. They were miles from Bomont and light years away from the stupid law about dancing. Ariel and Rusty went straight for the dance floor, but Willard hung back along the edges.

"Aren't you going to dance?" Ren asked.

Willard waved him off. "Nah. I'll just watch you guys."

"We drove all this way," Rusty insisted. "You're just going to stand around like a dork the whole time?"

He flashed an uncomfortable smile. "Well, darlin', I'd rather be a dork than a dancing dork."

Rusty's disappointment was obvious as Ariel pulled her onto the dance floor, but Ren wasn't about to let this go. His friend was missing a golden opportunity.

"What are you doing?" Ren asked once the girls were out of earshot.

Willard was embarrassed. "Look. I can't dance. At all. I mean *at all*. Not pretty."

Ren pointed to the dance floor. "But it's line dancing. It's a white man's dream. Simple steps, man. Simple."

Maybe there was a way to get Willard out there. Ren saw a woman teaching line dance steps to a small group of people off to the side of the dance floor. Probably an instructor the bar hired to help bring people in. It was the perfect solution.

"All right. Come over here." Ren grabbed Willard and pulled him to the corner.

The instructor was ready for them with a smile on her face by the time Ren reached her. "Excuse me, miss?"

"Y'all need to learn some new steps?" she asked.

That was when Willard caught on to what was happening. "Aw, shit-howdy. You're gonna drop me off at the day care while you go boogie with the girls?"

Ren stood firm. "Learn a box step or two and meet us out there. I have faith in you."

Ren joined the girls out on the dance floor. The song might be new to him, but the beat was universal. He and the girls fell in line with the other dancers, boots stomping, hands clapping. Every now and then a shout of "yee-haw" sprang from the crowd.

It felt great to move again. To just go wild, even with the tightly choreographed steps. Having a beautiful girl on each side of him didn't hurt, either. Willard didn't look like he was having nearly as much fun over with the beginners.

The music changed again and the lines of dancers broke up into a rowdy free-for-all. This was the kind of dancing that Ren liked. No structure. No rules.

He moved dangerously close to Ariel. As good as she was and as wild as she seemed, she was surprisingly inhibited when he turned to her. He shouted out some encouragement, moving suggestively, enticing her to join him. And she did. Slowly at first, but then she matched him move for move, twirling and gyrating, letting the music take control.

Ren saw Rusty leaving the dance floor out the corner of his eye. While they danced, Willard had quit his lessons and managed to get himself a beer.

"Come on! It's fun, Willard!" she shouted over the music, making a second attempt to coax him onto the dance floor.

He held up his beer. "I don't drink and dance. You go ahead."

Rusty swiped his hat right off his head. She put it on and danced seductively, trying to sway him into following her.

Willard was not amused. "Hey, give that back. I got hat head, darlin'. Come on."

His concern turned to something else entirely as her dance got more suggestive. She poured on the sexy, making that hat look better than it ever could on top of his head. Then suddenly, she jumped back into the group of dancers, leaving him behind.

"Hey, come on back!" he shouted after her.

Rusty was beside Ren and Ariel, but they barely noticed. They were too busy with each other. Hands roamed over their clothing as they moved to the music, forging a connection they didn't have the last time they danced.

Rusty was getting into it, too, dancing with some big cowboy. He couldn't move nearly as well as she did, but it didn't look like she minded very much. At first, she enjoyed the attention as he put his arm around her, but then his hand started creeping south.

"Aw, hell no!" Willard pushed his way through the crowd of dancers. "Hey, that's my girl you're groping."

"Willard, we were just dancing," Rusty protested.

Willard looked at her. "And what are you doin' dancing

with another man while you're wearing my hat? That's bad form, Rus," Willard said. "That's disrespect."

The big cowboy grabbed Rusty's purse out of her hands and shoved it into Willard's gut. "Here, pal. Why don't you hold the girl's purse and go get me a beer?"

Willard's face turned red. "I got a better idea. Why don't I kick your teeth in and grin doin' it?"

"Willard," Rusty said. "No fights. You don't even know this guy."

But Willard wasn't listening. "If you can count this high, I'm giving you to the count of three to get out of my face. One . . ."

The cowboy decked Willard before he even reached two.

Rusty screamed. "Willard!"

The cowboy grabbed Rusty by the arm. "C'mon, darlin'. Ditch the hayseed and party with a real man."

Rusty grabbed a bottle off the tray of a passing wait-ress and smashed it into the cowboy's head. "Animal!" she yelled as he went down hard.

Ren and Ariel had made their way toward their friends, and they realized they needed to get out of there before this little spat escalated. "You get Rusty," Ren told Ariel. "I'll get the big softy."

Ren helped his friend to his wobbly feet while Ariel pulled Rusty off the dance floor. Ariel had a hard time keeping hold of her friend. The girl was swearing up and down at the guy who hurt Willard. It was beginning to look like the shy flirtation she and Willard had going on had just turned into a full-blown romance.

They escaped to the parking lot, ready to make a break for it if the cowboy's friends came after them. After a minute or so, they seemed to be in the clear. Laughing, Rusty pulled a handkerchief out of her purse to staunch the blood flowing from Willard's nose. "I'm proud of you, Willard. You didn't fight."

"Didn't get a chance to, with you fighting all my battles." He took the handkerchief away from his face. "Shit-howdy, is this noticeable?"

Ren recoiled and the girls squealed. It took another five minutes for the nosebleed to stop, but by then it didn't look that bad, all things considered.

They squeezed back into the small car and headed toward home. All in all, it was for the best that their evening ended early. Ren didn't need another strike against him for bringing Ariel home after curfew again.

The ride back was full of silly conversations about the latest celebrity scandals. Ren enjoyed just talking about things that were crazy and wild and boring and normal. It was fun. But he noticed a sudden break in the chatter as they turned onto a bridge not far from Bomont.

"This bridge gives me the creeps," Willard said as they crossed the river.

"Willard." Rusty shushed him sharply under her breath, which just made it more noticeable.

"Oh," Willard said. "Sorry."

"What?" Ren asked.

"This is Crosby Bridge," Ariel said softly.

Ren couldn't make the connection. He'd crossed this bridge coming into town on the bus a few months back, and a couple times since then. Nothing about it stood out to him.

"After a homecoming game a bunch of kids were out partying. Drinking and dancing." Ariel had a catch in her voice. "Somehow, on their way home, they lost control and went head-on into a truck. Killed them all."

Ren pieced it together. He never realized that accident had happened on this bridge.

"They were all seniors," Willard continued for her. "Two of them were all-state. Ronnie Jamison and . . ."

"And my brother, Bobby." Ariel finished his sentence. She looked at Ren. "You would have liked him," she continued. "I looked up to him. He was my hero. But now whenever I think of him, I think about this bridge."

They continued the rest of the way in silence.

Chapter 17

They were the youngest people in the room by at least two decades. Ren, Woody, and Willard felt noticeably out of place sitting in the back row of the city council chamber among the people requesting permits or petitioning to have potholes filled.

The meeting mostly focused on civic business—the kinds of things that Ren never really worried about, but knew someone had to be responsible for. Principal Dunbar was finishing up that official business with a decree that the cost of a dog license would now rise from ten to fifteen dollars. It was exciting stuff. He even banged a gavel.

Woody leaned over to Ren. "They just finished. If you were gonna make your move, this is when you'd do it."

Principal Dunbar banged his gavel again. Ren could tell the man got a kick out of that part of the job. "It is at this time that we will take any new business or concerns. Just come down to the podium and state your name and address."

Woody and Willard looked at Ren. This was going to be a bigger challenge than he'd anticipated. He hadn't expected there'd be an audience, that he'd have to stand up in front of a microphone and announce his intentions. He especially didn't like bringing Uncle Wes into it by giving his address. Not that everyone in the room didn't already know who Ren was.

"Anyone?" Principal Dunbar asked. "Anyone?"

Ren wasn't sure what he'd been thinking. It was one thing to take on the council, but he was also challenging Ariel's father. If he did that in front of everyone, it could ruin whatever was forming between him and Ariel. He wasn't so sure a dance was worth risking that.

The gavel decided for him. Principal Dunbar slammed it down on the desk one last time and called the meeting to an end.

Despite his misgivings, Ren knew what he had to do. He left Willard and Woody in the back of the room and hurried to catch up with the departing council members, stopping Principal Dunbar and Reverend Moore as they came down the stairs.

"Reverend Moore?"

They turned to face him. No going back now. "Ren McCormack," he said, introducing himself. "Wesley's nephew."

Reverend Moore extended his hand out of politeness. "Yes, Ren. I know who you are."

"I'm sure you do," Ren said as he shook the man's hand. "Wes told me you two had a talk."

The statement made Reverend Moore uncomfortable. "That was a conversation between him and me," the reverend said. "It wasn't meant for your ears."

Which basically meant it was okay for the adults to talk about him behind his back. *Nice.* "Yeah. There's a lot of that going on in this town," Ren said. "What's that saying? The one about children?"

Principal Dunbar jumped in. "That they're better seen than heard."

Nice message from a man who made a living working with kids. Ren let it slide. "Well, I just wanted you to know that I'm starting a petition to challenge the ordinance prohibiting public dancing. I just wanted to . . ." He wanted to do a lot of things, actually, but none of them were right to say at the moment. "I just wanted to make myself clear."

He handed Roger one the flyers he'd made. It read OPPOSE THE DANCE BAN in big letters that filled the page. Ren walked away before his nerves got the best of him. He heard the reverend tell Roger that they should just ignore him. "He's just one kid," Reverend Moore added. "What can he do?"

It was a good question. Ren still didn't have an answer.

It was nothing more than a petition, but Ren had started something he had to see through to the end, no matter what happened. No turning back.

"Showdown with the preacher man," Woody said when Ren joined them.

Willard was suitably impressed, and let Ren know it with a "Shit-howdy."

But Ren wasn't having any of it. "Listen to me," he said, pointing a finger at Willard. "If I have to stand up in front of that city council and make my case, then you're going to learn how to dance."

"Okay, okay," Willard said. "You got me. We'll get together this weekend."

Ren grabbed him by the collar. "Uh-uh. Now." He and Woody marched Willard out of the council chambers and into the car to take them across town. Willard whined the entire way there about being abducted. Like a petulant child, he refused to even get out of the car when they pulled into Ren's garage. Ren had to coax his friend out by dangling an ice cream cone in front of him.

Willard firmly planted himself in the corner of the garage while Ren and Woody walked him through some basic moves to the sounds of the hip-hop emerging from the VW's speakers.

They started out with some easy stuff, nothing too fancy—just teaching him how to step to the beat. Willard nodded along out of rhythm while his ice cream dripped on the floor. "You all look so cute dancing together," he said. "But shouldn't you be closer? Like hugging each other? Woody, just take Ren's hand and lead. Be the man."

Ren stamped his foot. "Hey. No jokes. We're in school right now. We're schooling you."

"That's right," Woody agreed. "You go on and run your mouth, but this here is for your benefit. Not ours."

Willard got up with his ice cream cone and did a vulgar shimmy, spraying drops of vanilla ice cream around.

Ren rolled his eyes. "All right. Watch my feet and try to do what they do."

The beat pounded out of the speakers and Ren stomped his feet along with it. Just a simple right-left move. But when Willard tried it, he nearly took out a pile of car parts tripping over himself, giving Woody a case of the giggles.

"You're not being too helpful." Willard sounded more upset than Ren imagined he would be. Maybe he was taking this more seriously than he let on.

"I think the key word here is *hopeless*," Woody said to Ren.

But he wasn't about to give up. "If you can't learn to dance to *this* beat, then you can't learn to dance." Ren moved his feet again, emphasizing each word along with the beat. "This is primal. It's basic four-four."

Willard threw up his hands in defeat and left the garage. "Okay. Officially, I'm over this."

Ren called after him. "You know we've got better things to do than give you dance lessons."

"Why are you trying so hard?" Woody asked. "If he don't want to dance, you can't make him."

"Being scared of something and not wanting to do it are two different things," Ren said. He'd been scared of a lot of things in his life, but he didn't have much choice in whether or not he did them. He could tell Willard wanted to learn to dance. Especially with the way he watched Rusty at the club the other night. He just had to get over his fears.

The same way Ren was going to have to get up in front of the city council and make a presentation—something that would convince a bunch of old guys to see things from his point of view. To remember what it was like when they were his age and wanted to go out and have some fun. If he couldn't even convince his friend to have a good time, he didn't have a chance with the council.

Ren turned off his iPod, but music still filled the air. A new remix version of the song "Let's Hear It for the Boy" came from the backyard, along with the off-key voices of Amy, Sarah, and their friends.

The girls had set up a makeshift stage on the concrete slab where an old shed used to be. Their pink Superstar Sing-Along CD player sat before an audience of dolls and teddy bears, ready for a concert. Woody called Ren over to the window. "You gotta see this," he said.

Ren saw that the girls weren't alone. Watching their

performance from a distance, Willard made an earnest attempt to dance along with them. It wasn't pretty, but he kept up with them as they sang and danced around.

"Wonder if Uncle Wes can get fined for that," Ren said.

"I think Willard should definitely be fined for it," Woody added.

But Willard had caught the dancing bug, and Ren wasn't about to let him lose it. Every free moment he had over the next few weeks, Ren taught Willard how to move. They started at the cotton mill, with other unskilled dancers surrounding Willard in the saddest line dance Ren ever saw.

That was the secret to getting Willard to dance. He was too embarrassed to strut his stuff in front of people who knew what they were doing, like Ren and Woody. But throw in some little girls who only did the basic steps or some blue collar workers who didn't care how bad they looked, and he actually started to learn.

Once he got more comfortable, they took the show on the road. Now that there was some distance from the dance incident at the drive-in that got Ren in trouble with Reverend Moore, music was back in full force outside the diner. Willard was getting good at moving his feet, but the rest of his body was a big mess.

"Just bounce," Woody said as he and some of his cousins tried to add swagger to the moves. "Gangstas don't dance. They bounce. Get gangsta, Willard."

Willard got better with each lesson, but his best work was always with Sarah and Amy. The girls encouraged him, taking their role in his lessons very seriously, showing him choreography they'd seen in music videos online.

While Ren was building up Willard's dancing confidence, he was also working on his case for the council. He snuck into the high school copy room to run off extra flyers to spread the word, taping them up around the school and all over town in the places he knew other kids hung out.

A few times he returned to places he'd posted the flyers and found them gone, but he didn't get discouraged. He just put them up again, doubling up the tape. If people were going to take his stuff down, he was going to at least make it harder for them to do it.

Everywhere Ren went, Willard was with him, listening to his iPod and bouncing to the music. It got so bad that at one point Willard was practicing dance steps while holding the defensive line during football practice. Coach Guerntz was not pleased. "Willard, what the hell are you doing? Give me two miles! Move it!"

* * * * *

Willard slipped in one last little box step before hitting the track to work off his punishment. With every move that Willard mastered, Ren felt the dance get closer to reality. But it was only going to happen if he convinced the council to see things his way; for that, he needed to come up with one hell of a speech.

Getting people to sign the petition was the easy part—most everyone in the senior class eligible to vote had lined up to add their names. Some were dying for a formal dance, while others were just tired of all the rules that prevented them from having any fun. A few students, like Chuck's friends, only signed it as a joke. But even after Ren erased all the "Batman" and "Spider-Man" signatures, he still had more than enough names on the petition to challenge the law.

If only he could get some of those people to write his speech for him!

In school, oral reports were never Ren's thing. His mind always wandered, wondering what the teacher was thinking or what his friends were whispering about in front of him—and that was just for a simple book report. This speech had to convince the council, motivate his friends, and change the minds of everyone in town who was against him. That was a lot to ask.

Ren tore the top sheet off his notepad, crumpling his first draft into a ball. *Crap.* He tossed it into the small trash can in the corner of his bedroom.

"Hey." Aunt Lulu stood in the doorway. "Was that a three-pointer or just a two?"

Ren sat up on his bed. "That's a no-pointer." He put the blank notepad down beside him. It was as good a time as any for a break. "Getting names on a petition is one thing. Writing a speech is something else. It's hard."

Lulu sat beside him and pulled a folded-up piece of paper out of her pocket. It was one of his flyers, covered in stickers of unicorns and Barbie dolls. "I see you've enlisted my daughters in your campaign."

He took the sheet, happy to see that along with the stickers it was also filled with names. "I'm sorry about that."

"No need to apologize. This family could use some activism."

Ren wasn't sure *everyone* in the family would agree. "What about Uncle Wesley? He seems worried."

Lulu sighed. "Well, he's a car salesman trying to sell cars in the middle of a recession. He's all about worry. He worries about income. About what his customers might think. But that's what grown-ups do. We worry. That's not your job."

He had to disagree. That had been Ren's main job for the past five years. It was all he could do up in Boston. Worry about his mom's health. Worry about paying the bills. Worrying had become second nature.

"Why is this dance so important to you?" Lulu asked.

That was the whole problem with this speech. He couldn't figure out a way to put the answer to that question into words. "For city and school officials to make a general ban based on fear is an infringement on my—"

Lulu held up a hand. "Whoa! Save all that for your speech. I want to know why this is important to *you*."

Ren never really thought about it that way. The dance ban was just *wrong*. It was wrong for everyone, not just him. But why was the whole situation getting to him so badly?

Ren began to piece together his answer. "When Dad left . . . I wasn't really surprised. Even as a kid, I never felt like I could depend on him. It was just me and Mom, you know? She was the strong one."

Lulu nodded. That wasn't a big secret in the family.

"So when she got sick," he continued, "it was my turn to be strong. I thought that if I worked hard enough, if I listened to her doctors and did everything they told me, maybe we could turn it around. Maybe she could pull through." Back then, it was always easier to fool himself into thinking he had control over the situation. "All that effort was for nothing. I couldn't change a thing."

He took a deep breath. "But this . . . I'm thinking I could really do something. I could really do something for *me* this time. And maybe have a shot at making a change. That's all I want. Just a shot. Otherwise . . . I'm just going to disappear like everyone else."

Lulu held a hand out to Ren. "May I have that petition, please?"

Ren smiled and passed the decorated flyer back to her with his pen. She held the paper down on her leg and gently added her name. "You've got my vote, Ren McCormack."

Lulu handed the form back to Ren, kissed him on the forehead, and left him to gather his thoughts. It wasn't the solution to his creative-writing problem, but knowing he had at least some of his family's support meant something to him.

Actually, it meant a *lot*.

Chapter 18

"Aren't you going to say anything?"

They were in Chuck's truck bed, just sitting. Ariel had her arms wrapped around her knees. She'd expected Chuck to yell at her. Fight for her. Do *something*. It was the silence that killed her. It proved what she already suspected—that he didn't even care.

"You're not telling me anything I don't know," he said. "I've got eyes and ears."

His blasé tone made it all worse. She never thought she was in love with him, but she did believe that she at least mattered. "Well, I wanted to tell you myself."

"First you're into race car drivers. Now you're into dancin' gymnasts? You crack me up." He leaned across the truck bed. "I've seen the way you been lookin' at him. Just waiting for the right moment to dumb down and throw yourself at him."

Ariel pushed him away. If there was anyone she ever dumbed down for, it was Chuck. "I'm so sick of you treating me like dirt!"

She jumped out of the truck, but Chuck followed. *Now* he was angry. "Hey! Is that what I been doing? Treating you like just another pit row hussy? I thought that's what you came here to be. Being a preacher's daughter don't give you a pass on acting like a slut."

Ariel slapped him to shut him up. She pounded on him with her fists. His words hit close to home. She had been that way, acting out. The difference was that Chuck played along—he used her the way she let him. Not like Ren . . .

Her blows were wild, crazed. He ducked and dodged until he managed to lift her at the waist and slam her into the ground with a force that made her shout with pain.

Chuck leaned over her. "I treated you decent. More than you deserved."

Ariel stayed on the ground as Chuck got back into his truck and started the ignition, pulling out from under the bleachers. She couldn't let it end this way, letting Chuck think he'd made his point. That he won. Chuck had to circle the bleachers to reach the exit, so Ariel ran out the other side. She was waiting for him with a crowbar she'd grabbed from a pile of tools. She slammed it into the hood of the truck.

Dirt flew as Chuck skidded to a stop and jumped out, screaming at her. "Hey! *HEY!* Goddammit!"

Ariel couldn't stop herself. Each blow to the truck was payback for how she'd let him use her. For how she'd let him treat her. She took out a headlight.

Chuck punched her arm until she dropped the crowbar. Defenseless now, Chuck smacked her, with the full force of his body behind it. She fell down in the dirt, sobbing, holding her face.

"Walk your ass back home to Daddy."

Dirt and gravel sprayed Ariel as Chuck peeled out, leaving her behind—alone.

* * * * *

She couldn't call her father. Not like this. It would be the end of everything. Maybe Rusty. If she could find her phone. Where the hell was her phone?

"What in God's name . . ."

Ariel cringed. She knew that voice. Someone else she didn't want to see.

"Ariel, girl, are you all right?"

Ariel winced as she sat up. "Leave me alone, Caroline. Just go."

But the woman didn't move. "Look, I know we ain't friends, but I'm getting you out of here, so you just shut up and come with me, okay?"

Ariel thought she heard something she could trust in Caroline's voice, if not in her words. The woman had been around this track for a long time. Maybe she was used to this kind of thing. She carefully helped Ariel to her feet and got her into a car.

Caroline always treated Ariel badly, but she was the best thing to happen to her that afternoon. Ariel didn't want to say anything, and Caroline didn't want to hear anything. She drove in silence, taking the directions when she got back into town. Ariel knew her mother would be at the church that afternoon, so that's where she went.

She thanked Caroline and sent her away, knowing if they ever ran into each other again, they would never mention that this happened. If only she could be so lucky with her parents.

* * * * *

Ariel saw her daddy's secretary, Mrs. Allyson, first. The woman took her inside the church and sprung into action. The next thing Ariel knew, Momma was holding her. She barely had the chance to start her story before she heard tires screeching out front. Daddy's voice came from the hall. He was suddenly in front of her.

"That son of a bitch."

It was the first time Ariel had ever heard her father curse. But she had no idea who he was talking about. He didn't know about Chuck, did he?

"Careful, Daddy," Ariel said. "You're in church." She couldn't imagine how she looked to him. She'd only caught a glimpse of her reflection in Caroline's car. It wasn't pretty. The black eye was already forming.

"Did Ren McCormack do this to you?"

Ren? How on Earth could he think Ren would do something like this? "Answer me!" he yelled.

Ariel flinched. She couldn't even speak.

"Shaw! Calm down." Her mom was just as angry, but she was trying to be reasonable. Ariel always appreciated that. No matter how bad the situation, her momma always kept a cool head. Bobby was like that, too.

"Our daughter's been assaulted, Vi," her father insisted. "And he's going to pay for this."

"An eye for an eye." Ariel found her voice in her own anger. It was just like Daddy. Ready to shut someone down before he knew the situation. The truth didn't matter to him anymore. It was all about appearances.

"I warned you about him!"

Ariel looked up at him. The bruise must have been bad. He could barely meet her gaze. "For someone who's supposed to look into people's hearts and souls, you are blind as a bat."

Daddy ignored her and turned to Vi. "I want that guy in handcuffs."

"I can see how that works for you," Ariel fumed. "Just blame it all on Ren. Just like you did with Bobby."

Reverend Moore was shocked. "What? What are you talking about?"

In the silence that followed, Ariel let her parents see

her cry for the first time in years. "Bobby spent his whole life trying to make you proud. He got good grades. Went to church on Sunday. But God help him, 'cause he made one mistake. Now nobody remembers good things about Bobby. Just that damn accident."

Ariel saw that Momma heard what she was saying, but Daddy still needed convincing. "It's because of *Bobby* that there's no school dance. It's because of Bobby that we've got this curfew." Ariel's voice rose with each accusation. "Bobby's to blame for all this."

Daddy wasn't having it. "You will lower your voice and keep a civil tone."

Momma did what she always did. She deflected. "Ariel, let's not do this here."

"Why not?" Ariel asked. "Isn't this my church? Isn't this where we're supposed to talk about our problems?"

The dam finally burst. All the pain, the hurt—everything she'd locked inside, everything that had been building up, came flooding out of her. Confession was good for her soul. "I've been . . . lost. I've been losing my mind. But you don't see. You don't care."

"Of course we care," Daddy said. "And I don't expect for you to understand all that has been intended to protect you and shield you—"

Ariel cut him off. She wasn't in the mood for his condescending attitude. "Oh, stop it! I hate it when you talk down to me like some child."

His raised his voice. "Whether you like it or not, young lady, you *are* my child."

"I'm not even a virgin!"

The words were out of her mouth before she could stop them. She wanted something to shock him into listening to her. To make him hear.

Daddy was beside himself with rage. "Don't you talk like that in here!"

"What are you going to do? Pass another law?" she shouted back at him. "You just about outlawed everything. That sure as hell didn't keep 'em out of my panties."

Reverend Moore slapped Ariel across the face. It was a shock beyond anything she'd ever experienced. It was just as shocking for her father.

"Shaw!" her mother yelled.

Ariel was defiant. "Well, let's go string up the guy who blacked my eye. Because we don't hit girls in Bomont. Right, Daddy?"

He was shaking. "Ariel. Please. I didn't mean to." He moved toward her, but Ariel ran out of the room. She couldn't deal with it. It was all too much.

"No!" she heard her momma say to her father. "You stay here! I mean it!"

Momma called out for her, but Ariel couldn't stop. Not till she got outside, away from her daddy's church. Away from his judging eyes.

"Ariel, please," Momma pleaded.

She finally stopped in the parking lot, trying to calm herself as her momma approached. She did everything wrong. Made everything worse.

"Momma, I can't go back," she said. "Not now. I can't—"

"It's okay, baby," Vi said, wrapping her arms around her daughter. "None of this is your fault. None of it."

But Ariel wasn't so sure. She'd let it all spiral out of control. She'd let her life get so crazy. "It's not Ren's, either," she said. "He didn't do this. He would never do this."

"I know," Vi said. "I'm a pretty good judge of character."

Ariel cringed. Her momma knew nothing about her character.

"Don't you dare do that," Vi said, as if reading Ariel's mind. "I know you, girl. I know you better than you know yourself. I may have missed some things, but that doesn't mean you're not my baby anymore. That you're not the same good girl I raised. I'm just sorry I haven't been there for you more. I promise that will change."

"And Daddy?"

"He's a good man," she said. "He just lost his way."

Ariel wanted to make a joke. A snide remark. But she just let her mother hold her.

"Come on," Vi said. "Let me take you to Rusty's. I think you need a friend right now. Maybe even more than you need your parents."

"I'll always need you, Momma," Ariel said.

Vi kissed her daughter's forehead. "Not half as much as I need you."

* * * * *

Ariel's father was a broken man. As broken as the rusted old swing set in the backyard he'd been meaning to tear down for years. He'd been broken ever since that horrible night Officer Herb came knocking at his door. But it was no excuse for what he'd done to his daughter. He could barely look his wife in the eyes when she came up to him. "Where is she?"

"She's staying at Rusty's," Vi replied.

The clouds were full and dark overhead. Rain was on the way. "I've never hit anyone in my life. I don't know what came over me."

"That's where you two are alike," she said. "You deal with your pain in extremes."

Vi sat on the swing beside her husband. The metal squealed from years of neglect. "Right after Bobby died," she said, "I was, of all things, shopping for headstones. They told me that the stone would take three weeks, but the engraving process would take ten months. I asked them, 'Why so long? My son's already in the ground.' They told me it was the cemetery's policy to wait a year before any engraving is allowed."

That explained something Shaw had always wondered. He'd never been able to bring himself to ask. Much as he prayed for Bobby silently on his own and out loud in church, he had a hard time visiting his son's grave. It was unfair, but he'd left all that business up to Vi when it happened. He was focused on other things.

"They do this because families, in their grief and suffering, tend to say too much," Vi explained. "When what they really require is time to collect their thoughts. Time to heal. To mourn and remember."

Shaw felt like he was still healing, that he'd be healing forever. It was harder now that Ariel opened up the old wounds—wounds that maybe needed reopening to heal properly.

"I know we were trying to protect our children," Vi said. "But these laws. It was too much. Too soon."

Shaw's thoughts went to the same place they always did: to the other children. The ones in the car with Bobby. The ones who weren't behind the wheel. "There were others who lost their lives. I felt an obligation—"

"Your obligation was to our daughter." Her voice was gentle but firm. "And by turning to your congregation, somehow you turned away from her." Vi got off the swing so she could face her husband directly. "It's been twenty-one years now I've been a minister's wife. I've been supportive. I've been silent. I still believe you're a wonderful preacher." She paused. "But it's the one-on-one where you need a little work."

Vi left her husband alone, staring at the broken swing set.

Chapter 19

The bruise on Ariel's face looked worse in the shadows of the railcar. She'd covered it up as best she could with makeup, but Ren still saw it under the surface. It was all he could do to contain his anger. "Your old man may be wrong about a lot, but tossing Chuck in prison sounds like a good idea to me."

"I just want it all behind me," she said. "I feel like an idiot."

Ren had already told her to stop blaming herself. Yeah, she'd gone crazy out at the track; she should feel bad about that. But it didn't give Chuck the right to do what he did. Not by a long shot.

"I got something for you." Ariel reached into her bag and retrieved a worn-out children's Bible.

Ren took the book in his hands. "A Bible?"

"It's not just any Bible. It's mine. Had it since I was

seven." She opened the inside flap, revealing her name written in childlike cursive. She thumbed through it, showing some underlined passages to Ren. "I've marked a few pages for you. Thought you might need some help going up against the city council."

As he read the items she underlined, his enthusiasm grew. "Hey, this is great." Each line was exactly what he needed. "This is . . . this is perfect!"

Ariel looked up at him, proud of herself for helping him however she could. "You said you'd kiss me someday."

The Bible was suddenly forgotten. Ren smiled at her. "Yeah."

For the first time since he'd met her, Ariel was suddenly shy. Unsure of herself. It made her even more adorable. "You think that someday could be today?" she asked.

Ren answered by pressing his lips against hers. The kiss was slow and gentle—the kind that made them both feel less alone. Sweet and innocent, not hot with passion. There'd be time for that later. Not now, while they both had their hands on a Bible.

* * * * *

When he dropped her off, he walked her to the door like a gentleman. They shared one last quick kiss and she went inside. As he left her, he felt like he could take on the whole world. The city council and Chuck Cranston didn't stand a chance!

Ren's excitement kept him up most of the night as he

prepared his speech for the council and reviewed the Bible passages Ariel had selected. He didn't know if it was all the ammunition he'd need, but it was a great starting point.

Time flew faster than it had since he arrived in Bomont. Suddenly, it was two days later, and his uncle was taking him to the council meeting. He blinked, and they were at the city council chamber.

Teenagers outnumbered the adults two to one as everybody entered the large room. Impressive, since many of the teens hadn't even known for sure where the chamber was until they asked Ren. It was also terrifying.

It was bad enough that he was going to have to get up in front of the entire council and the regular audience—but now the full scope of this undertaking was weighing on him. His classmates were here to support him because they wanted a dance as badly as he did, maybe even more so. They were all probably too young to fully appreciate what they'd lost three years ago.

It was Uncle Wes, Aunt Lulu, and the girls who made Ren the most nervous. He didn't want to let them down. Wes had made sure to remove the neon sign at his car lot the other day. He'd been ignoring Roger's request since the councilman mentioned it in front of Ren more than two months ago, but it came down right after Ren told his uncle what he was doing.

Ariel was in the aisle with her mother. The bruise on her face was still noticeable, but not as bad. Ren had to push thoughts of the attack from his mind as she approached. He had too much to worry about already.

"Are you nervous?" Ariel asked.

"I'm friggin' terrified," he said under his breath. He didn't need anyone around him hearing that—the adults who were against him or the kids supporting him.

"Let me give you something to think about while you're up there." She unbuttoned one of the snaps on her blouse. "It's just for you to see." Another snap came undone. Ren checked around to make sure no one was looking. What was she doing? The rest of the snaps opened quickly as she flashed him the tank top she wore underneath. It read: "Dance Your Ass Off."

"That's sweet," Ren said as she quickly buttoned back up.

"I don't make T-shirts for just anybody. You're special." She kissed him lightly on the cheek. "Give 'em hell, Ren McCormack."

Ariel joined her mother and Rusty, who had been saving seats. It was nearly standing room only in the chamber. Ren went to his own seat next to Wes. Amy had taken special pride in keeping it safe for him. Willard, Woody, and Etta were in the row behind him. For the moment, Ren was safe in the cocoon of family and friends.

Not everyone was on his side, though. Mr. Parker and Officer Herb were there, too. Both of them eyed Ren as if they expected him to break the law at any moment—to light up a joint, or who knows what else.

Willard tapped his shoulder. "What's your secret plan? You gonna get up and dance?"

Ren cracked a nervous smile. "Wish it were that easy."

The gavel dropped as Principal Dunbar called the meeting to order.

The proceedings were endless, longer than even the last meeting Ren attended. The council went through each item on the agenda with excruciatingly slow deliberation, as if they hoped to bore the teens into leaving. To their credit, not one of Ren's supporters abandoned the room.

"Motion carried," Principal Dunbar said with another bang of the gavel. "Trash day will be moved to Wednesday and be limited to two containers."

There was a pause as the principal looked out over the crowd. "And now we can consider any new business," Principal Dunbar said. "But before we begin, I want to remind all you kids that we are conducting an official meeting. Official town business. And that means no disturbances will be tolerated." Amy and Sarah sat a little straighter beside Ren, as if they wanted it known that they took this very seriously.

"The floor is now open."

Here we go.

Ren stood, knowing that every single eye in the place was on him. He debated going to the microphone, but he wasn't sure he could make the long walk down the aisle on his wobbly legs.

"My name is Ren McCormack," he announced in a clear but shaky voice. "And I want to move, on behalf of most of the senior class of Bomont High School, that the . . . the law against public dancing within the town limits of Bomont be abolished."

The teens in the audience—and the two youngest children—erupted into cheers and applause. Roger was quick with his gavel. "We will have order here. You will not be warned again."

Reverend Moore leaned forward. "Roger, if I may address Mr. McCormack concerning this matter?"

Roger nodded his okay, and Ren braced for the battle to begin. It was the first time they'd seen each other since Ariel was hurt. Ren wondered if her father ever got word that he wasn't the one who had hit her.

The reverend spoke in a calm voice. "Besides the liquor and the drugs and the lewd behavior that always seems to accompany these unsupervised events, the thing that distresses me more, Ren, is the spiritual corruption. These dances . . . this music distorts young people's attitudes. It may seem funny to you, but I believe that dancing can be destructive. I believe that a celebration of certain music can be destructive. People in Boston may have a different opinion, but this is Bomont."

Not for the first time, Ren couldn't help but notice how people always seemed to put him down for being from that northern city.

"We are involved in our children's lives," the reverend

continued. "And we care. Ren, I'm afraid you're going to find that most of the people in our community are going to agree with me on this."

This time, the polite outbreak of applause came from many—but not all—of the adults in the room. Oddly, no one gaveled them into silence.

A councilwoman spoke up. "I believe a vote is in order on the motion."

Ren looked to his uncle and his friends. Was that it? That couldn't be it. "Excuse me," he said.

Roger ignored him. "Will all those opposed please indicate your vote with aye or . . ."

Ren tried to speak over him. "I still have some things I'd like to say on the issue."

"Hey, what's going on?" Wes asked as the teens in the audience added their voices to the confusion. "I thought Ren had the floor."

Roger pounded his gavel, shouting them down. "This meeting will come to order. Mr. McCormack, we have been more than patient with your intrusions. I would like to remind you that we speak for the town because we are from here."

A woman's hand went up to Ren's right. He realized it was Vi's hand. "Excuse me, Mr. Dunbar."

But the principal could not be stopped. He continued sputtering about the outrageousness of Ren's request.

"Roger, cut it out," Vi said sharply as she stood, shocking the principal and the rest of the council into silence.

In a softer voice, Vi added, "I think Mr. McCormack has the right to be heard."

The audience of supporters erupted again, letting the council know that there were people who grew up in Bomont who supported Ren. They'd chosen him to speak for them.

Ren stepped out of his row and moved to the podium with the microphone. He wanted to be sure that no one missed a word of this. He pulled the speech out of his pocket and unfolded it, smoothing the creases in the paper.

He'd lost a lot of sleep writing and rewriting the speech, making sure every word was perfect. But at that moment, being stared down by the council, he decided not to use it. He needed to look them in the eyes.

Ren folded the paper back up and made his case. "I wasn't here three years ago when tragedy hit this town. I know it's not my place to mourn the lives that were lost. I didn't know them. But that doesn't mean I don't think about them every day." He looked at Ariel. She smiled, sending all the silent encouragement that she could.

"I'm like a lot of the students at Bomont High," he continued. "I see that picture of them hanging on the wall at school every day. Each time I see their faces, I think about how precious life is. Because life can be taken away, so quickly. I know this firsthand, in my own way." There was a catch in his throat. Thinking about his mom always did that to him.

"I know it may be silly to most of you," Ren said, "this desire to have a dance where we could really, you know, go crazy. Just dance like idiots and let it all out. And maybe in the middle of all that dancing we might just touch each other." Ren laughed. Not in a condescending way—it was innocent. Genuine. "But there's nothing shameful about it. It's not sick. It's not a *sin*. Dancing is our way of celebrating life."

He pulled Ariel's Bible out from inside his jacket, holding it up so everyone could see. The pages she'd underlined were flagged with a rainbow of colorful sticky notes. Ren flipped to the first passage. "Aren't we told in Psalm 149, 'Praise ye the Lord. Sing unto the Lord a new song. Let them praise his name in the dance.'"

He paused to let those words sink in to the council and everyone else. Ren couldn't help but notice that Reverend Moore shared a look with his wife. "If any of you brought your Bible, like I did," Ren said, "please turn to the Book of Samuel, 6:14." He flipped to the next sticky note and read, "'David danced before the Lord with all his might. Leaping and dancing before the Lord.'" He turned to Reverend Moore. "Celebrating his love for God, celebrating his love for life—with *dancing*. I mean, if God said it, and we believe it, doesn't that settle it?"

Ren turned to the audience behind him, hoping to bring them along with him. "Ecclesiastes assures us that 'There is a time to every purpose under Heaven. A time to weep. A time to mourn. And there is a time to dance.'

This is our time." He let his message sink in for a moment, before turning back to the council. "Thank you."

He closed Ariel's Bible and walked back to his seat while everyone considered his words in silence.

Chapter 20

Shaw Moore's thoughts weighed heavily on him as he sat alone in his study. He'd voted his conscience this afternoon. He did what was best for the town. It was a tough decision, but he couldn't back down, no matter how his daughter felt about him because of it. He was getting used to the disappointment in her eyes.

Afterward, he came home and retired to his study, where he'd been ever since.

This was the place he typed up his sermons, the inspirational speeches he used to guide his congregation. To teach them the best way to live their lives. But what if he was wrong? What if he was as lost as his flock?

A shadow crossed into the light from the foyer. Vi was in the doorway, in her nightgown. It was later than he thought.

"You look tired," she said. "Come to bed."

Sleep would not affect his weariness. It was deeper, in his soul. "That's the second time I've sat in that council chamber and broke my daughter's heart. I'm losing her, Vi. Maybe I've already lost her."

His wife was about to say something, perhaps something to soothe him. But a knock on the front door caused them both to tense up. The last time someone knocked late at night, their world had been destroyed.

"Who could that be?" Vi asked.

Shaw tried not to hurry behind her as she stepped out of the room to open the front door. It was Roger Dunbar. Not quite the last person Shaw expected to see at that hour, but not the first, either. Roger stepped inside. He clearly had something on his mind.

"Hey, Shaw," he said. "I know it's late, but I thought you and I should talk." He finally noticed Vi had opened the door for him. "Sorry for the intrusion, Vi."

"What's wrong?" Shaw asked. His mind jumped to any number of potential problems. No telling what the teens from the council chamber were up to tonight, how they were reacting to the vote. He was trying not to condemn Ren McCormack without proof anymore, but he couldn't help but worry about any boy interested in his daughter.

Shaw wished he knew for certain that Ariel was still in bed.

"I can't help but be disturbed by the council vote,"

Roger said. "I think we need to circle the wagons first thing next week so we can get our priorities straight."

This didn't make any sense to Shaw. The votes had gone their way. Roger's voice had rung out the loudest. The ban on dancing would continue. "They voted in our favor, Roger. What more do you want?"

"It wasn't unanimous," Roger said, as if his reason for concern were obvious. "Not by a long shot. That's what troubles me."

"Maybe that's because Ren was making some sense," Vi interjected.

Roger turned to her. "I'm sorry, Vi, but that's where you and I have to disagree. That boy wasn't here three years ago. He doesn't know how ugly it got in this town before we united behind these laws." He focused back on Shaw. "Laws that you recommended, Shaw. And rightly so."

Shaw wasn't so sure about that any more. "But he makes a compelling argument," Shaw said. "Perhaps some of these restrictions are hurting more than they are helping."

Roger refused to relent. "You get to see these teenagers once a week, on Sunday. I deal with them every day. Let me tell you, these laws work. Young minds are highly impressionable. We have to be firm. It doesn't take long for corruption to take root."

"And how long is that, Roger?" Shaw asked. "About as long as it takes compassion to die?"

The conversation was growing unexpectedly tense.

Roger's anger rose. "I can't believe you are wavering on this. *Especially* you!"

"I'm not going to stand here and argue with you, Roger." Shaw tried to maintain his composure, but it wasn't easy. He was having a difficult enough time with this issue on his own; he didn't need Roger adding to his burden.

Vi placed a hand on her husband's shoulder. "Perhaps both of you should sleep on this and talk in the morning."

But Roger wasn't ready to let it go. "You're not the only one who lost someone on that bridge, Shaw." Reverend Moore was stunned. Roger had just crossed a line from which there was no return. "I stood shoulder to shoulder with you when everyone started blaming Bobby for that accident. You lost a son. I lost a daughter. And we still worked to bring this town together. I'll be damned if I'm going to let some cocky kid undo all that we made right."

Roger stormed out of the Moore home, slamming the door behind him.

Shaw stood rooted to the spot. How many people would throw his decisions back in his face? How many times would he be told he was wrong for doing what he thought was right?

He looked to his wife. If she ever turned on him, his life would be over.

Vi took his hand. "Come to bed."

Shaw let her guide him upstairs, turning out the lights

as they went. She'd planned to take him to their bedroom, but he wasn't ready to go yet. He needed to see his daughter. To know that she was safe.

He tapped lightly on the door, but there was no answer. No light shone through under the door. He didn't want to disturb her privacy, but he needed to know that she was there.

Quietly, he turned the knob and pushed the door open a crack—just enough so he could see her lying on the bed, looking so peaceful as she slept. He silently swore to Ariel that he would do right by her. Somehow, he'd figure out what it was that was wrong between them and find a way to heal.

Chapter 21

Ren was back at work, unloading mulch bags from the delivery truck and stacking them onto a pallet. He kind of enjoyed the repetitive work right now. Moving the heavy bags helped him work through his disappointment.

The odds had been against him when he walked into the council chamber. True, he did change some minds. The vote to repeal the law came close to carrying. Just not close enough.

His uncle tried to convince Ren that he'd started something. He got people talking, got them thinking. This was only the first step. Maybe by the time Sarah and Amy were in high school, the rules would make sense again. But Ren wasn't sure he'd still be in town to see it— even though he now had more reasons to stick around than he used to.

"You know you were railroaded," a voice said from behind him.

"Huh?" Ren was so lost in thought that he hadn't even heard Andy approaching.

"Shaw Moore walked into that meeting with the votes already in his pocket. You didn't have a prayer," Andy said. "So what happens now?"

Ren resumed his task. He didn't want to talk about it. "It's over. Nothing happens."

"What if it's not?" Andy asked. "What if you have your dance over in Bayson?"

Ren dropped a bag onto the pile and went back for another. "The point was to do it in Bomont. Bayson's what, thirty miles away?"

"Nope," Andy said as he walked away from the truck. "You're standing in it."

Ren dropped the mulch bag and followed Andy toward the road.

Andy pointed to something off in the distance. "You see that water tower? That's Bomont. But everything east of that is Bayson. That means the cotton mill. I figure if Bomont fire trucks can't come this far east, then neither can the long arm of the law."

Ren immediately recognized the flaw in that plan. "But what about the long arm of Reverend Moore?"

"Find a way to convince him that it won't be a 'spiritual corruption,' and maybe he'd think about it," Andy said, then headed back to work.

Ren attacked the mulch bags with new energy, finishing the job in half the time it would've taken before. Andy let him leave early, since the job was done and it was clear that Ren was now a man on a mission. A quick trip by the house to clean up, and Ren was soon on his way to the Bomont First Christian Church. According to Ariel, her daddy was there for the evening.

The lights were on in the church. He slipped in quietly, sitting in the shadows in one of the back pews. Reverend Moore was up at the pulpit, working on one of his sermons.

The man's voice echoed over the empty rows. "'I beheld and heard an angel flying through the midst of Heaven, saying with a loud voice, "Woe to the inhabiters of the Earth." And I saw a star fall from Heaven unto the Earth. And to an angel, a key was given. A key to the bottomless pit.'"

When Reverend Moore looked up from his text, he saw Ren's silhouette. It was almost as if the presence scared him. "Who . . . who's there? Show yourself."

Ren moved out of the shadows. This wasn't starting off well. "It's me. Ren McCormack."

The reverend seemed relieved, yet somehow disappointed. "Sometimes when I would work on my sermons, my son would sit right there in the back. I don't know what happened there."

"Yeah. With me it's grocery stores," Ren said.

"Pardon?"

"There's a lot of mothers in grocery stores. You get enough of them calling after their kids, and pretty soon you're going to come across one that sounds just like yours." He took a breath. "Sometimes I think I really hear her. I turn around, but . . ."

"I can't remember the last thing I said to my son," Moore admitted. The two of them had found something to bond over: the tragedies in their lives. "I can tell you what it wasn't. I know I didn't say 'I love you.'"

"It's not so easy when you've got time, either," Ren assured him. "You think you can say all the things you want to say, but . . . death is on its own clock."

"Yes, it is." For the first time, Reverend Moore looked at Ren with something like respect in his eyes.

It was now or never. Ren wasn't going to get a better moment. "I know the council voted against us having the dance. But that's not going to stop it. Andy Beamis has given us permission to hold it at his place."

The reverend was impressed, in spite of himself. "That's clever. His cotton mill isn't in our county."

"With your permission, I'd like to take Ariel," Ren said. "To the dance. I would never, ever do anything to hurt her or disrespect her. And I sure as hell wouldn't let anybody else . . . sorry. Didn't mean to swear in your church."

The reverend's smile lightened the mood slightly. "You wouldn't be the first."

"This dance means a lot to me," Ren explained. "But your daughter means more. So if you won't let her go, then I won't go, either. I know you've got to do what you've got to do, but . . . thanks for listening."

Reverend Moore heard what Ren was saying. He appeared to be rather touched, actually. "Thank you for . . . well, thank you."

Ren left the church without waiting for an answer. He didn't want to push it. He had said his piece; now it was best to let the reverend think about it. But he had hope. He most certainly had hope.

Chapter 22

Ariel didn't know what to do about her father. Things were bad between them. They had been since he slapped her—before that, even. The two of them managed to call a truce and move past it, but the house was filled with tension. It only got worse after he voted against the dance.

They weren't fighting, exactly. No screaming, no cursing; no nothing. They barely acknowledged one another's presence, aside from his repeated apologies for what he did. She wanted to apologize as well, for acting out, but she wasn't quite sure what she'd be apologizing for. She mostly felt like she should apologize to herself.

She and Ren shared a glance across the church aisle. At least that part of her life was working out pretty well. For the first time in forever, she was with a guy who wanted to be with *her*, not with the preacher's daughter.

Or maybe he wasn't the first, maybe she just needed to give people a chance. Regardless, she couldn't have picked a better one to start with.

A silent question passed between them. Something was wrong with Reverend Moore here, too. She wasn't the only one who noticed his extended silence. Everyone was looking at him.

Reverend Moore looked out at his congregation, almost as if he were surprised they were in front of him. "I'm standing here before you today with a troubled heart," he finally said.

"I've insisted on taking responsibility for your lives," he continued. "But I'm really just like a first-time parent, one who makes mistakes and learns from them as he goes along. And, like that parent, I find myself at that moment where I have to decide. Do I hold on? Or do I trust you to yourselves? Do I let go and hope that you've understood my lesson?"

His eyes fell on Ariel. This message was as much for her as it was the congregation. "If we don't start trusting our children, how will they ever become . . . trustworthy?"

Moore turned his attention to the other side of the aisle, where Ren sat. "I'm told that the senior class of Bomont High School has secured the use of a warehouse in nearby Bayson for a senior dance. Please join me in prayer that our Lord will guide them in their endeavors."

The silence that usually followed the reverend's call for prayers was broken by mumbles and whispers among the congregants. Rusty was busy chattering in Ariel's ear, but she didn't hear a word. She sat there, beaming with pride, focused on her two heroes: Ren and her father.

· · · · ·

The skies were clear and the sun shined brightly as a dozen ATVs and motorcycles crested the hill ahead of them. Ariel sat beside Ren in his VW Bug. Rusty had gone with Willard in his truck. Everyone could hear Willard's joyous hooting over the engine noise. They were the first wave in an army of volunteers heading out to the Beamis Cotton Mill.

Back in town, a surprising number of cars and trucks, all painted with school spirit signs reading BOMONT SENIORS and GO PANTHERS, passed by the principal. His students, and more than a few of their parents, were packed inside. Roger Dunbar watched as the Warnicker family pulled out of the car lot and headed out of town, probably going to catch up with their nephew.

Everyone was loud and raucous, honking horns and cheering out their windows. It was the kind of celebrating that usually only happened during a football game. It had been a while since the town had come together this way in unbridled excitement in the middle of a normal day. Part of him was afraid someone might cause an accident, not paying attention to where they were going.

But another part of him was starting to wonder if things could be like this more often.

Officer Herb watched as the cars sped past him on the road out of town, just slightly above the speed limit. Enough that he could stop them, but not enough that he should. It didn't take a genius to realize he'd be shouted down if he pulled anyone over. They were driving safely enough. Staying within the law. As long as nobody caused any harm, it was better to let them be.

A few miles down that very road, Andy Beamis opened the large barn doors to the mill's storage area. This was the place where things were dumped and forgotten. It was a big, cluttered space that needed a lot of attention if it was going to be ready for the dance. The large number of Bomont residents spilling in through the door had a real job ahead of them.

Someone cranked up the tunes and they all got busy cleaning. An assembly line of students passed the junk from hand to hand to clear out the building. Parents swept the floors. Even little Sarah and Amy Warnicker were at work, polishing the windows until sunlight came streaming through.

It took the better part of the day for all those people to get the large section of the mill emptied and cleaned, but the work had only begun. There was nothing festive about the wooden beams and peeling paint. That was going to take some more attention.

Etta pulled out some old lights she'd taken from her grandma's backyard patio. The woman had been thrilled to donate to the cause, telling her granddaughter about her senior dance many years ago. The lights weren't very fancy—just lightbulbs strung together in mason jars. But at night, they'd help make the old mill look magical.

Woody and his friends were on ladders, hanging curtains to hide the rattier parts of the mill and provide some private spaces for quieter conversation. The parents kept an eye on what they were doing, making sure that everything stayed open to the dance floor. No secret dark corners where anyone could get into trouble. Just because they supported the dance didn't mean they'd abandoned all their concerns.

Ren took it all in, surprised at how good it felt. It was just a dance. But somewhere along the way it had become more important than just having some fun. He did this for Bomont. He did it for Ariel.

She and Rusty were over in the corner with Rusty's little cousins, blowing up balloons. Well, that wasn't quite right. There were spending more time on breaks sucking in the helium to make funny voices. Rusty in particular was having fun with cartoon voices, entertaining the girls. But Ariel . . . she looked relaxed for the first time since he'd met her. Just having fun. Not a care in the world. It made her even more beautiful in Ren's eyes.

He had to laugh when the four girls started singing along with a Katy Perry song, sounding even squeakier with their helium voices than the pop singer did at her highest pitched.

"Hey, Willard!" Ren motioned for his friend to follow him over to the exhaust chute that kept the air circulating through the room.

"What is it, man?" Willard asked. "They need me on the disco ball."

"Just a sec. That can wait. I need your help." Ren pointed into the exhaust chute. "Check this out for me. Tell me what you see."

Like the naive guy he was, Willard did exactly what Ren asked. Once his head was lined up with the chute, Ren flipped a switch, sending a strong blast of air at Willard's face that blew his cowboy hat right off his head.

"Well, shit-howdy!" Willard exclaimed as the air blew him back. It gave Ren a great idea for later that night. Willard smacked him on the shoulder and got back to work. One last finishing touch to go.

The place looked better than Ren ever thought it could. He almost couldn't tell they were in an old mill, which was exactly the point of their hard work.

A cheer rang out as Uncle Wes came through the barn doors carrying a large cardboard box over his head like a trophy. He opened the box and pulled out a large disco ball. The mirrored ball passed from person to person all the way up to the table Willard stood on. He hooked it onto the ceiling, then struck a pose like John Travolta in *Saturday Night Fever*, cracking everyone up.

The work was done. The place was ready for the dance later that night, but no one was quite ready to leave just yet. With the music cranking, Ren grabbed his little cousins and started dancing. Ariel was quick to join them, pulling Rusty onto the dance floor with her. Wes and Lulu were next, showing the kids how it was done.

Soon everyone but Willard was on the floor, yet even he was tapping his toe to the beat. It was the first time in a long time any of these adults danced with their kids, and Ren still couldn't quite believe that he was the one who had made it happen.

· · · · ·

Things were more somber back in Bomont. Shaw Moore was outside his home on the rusted swing set again, staring at the empty swing beside him. He remembered back when Bobby and Ariel would play out here, screaming for him to push them higher and higher. Back when their daddy could do no wrong.

Shaw had done a lot wrong lately. Always with the best intentions, but best intentions are what they said lined the road to Hell. It was time he made amends with his children. *Both* his children.

After a quick stop, Shaw found himself at the Bomont cemetery, walking past the tombstones of the town ancestors. He headed for the newer section of the field, where the stonework was still fresh and the grass still dotted with flowers. He carried his own bouquet in his hands—wildflowers, to match the wildness he used to appreciate in his kids.

Shaw stood before the grave of his son. ROBERT MOORE, 1990—2007. OUR BELOVED SON AND BROTHER.

He placed the bouquet beneath his son's name and said a little prayer asking for forgiveness. But not from God—he needed absolution from the child whose memory he had honored the wrong way. Shaw promised his son that he would do better. He would start by delivering the other flowers in his hand: the corsage for his daughter.

Chapter 23

The black bow tie was more of a struggle than Ren expected, but he won out in the end. He gave it one last tug and slipped into his maroon jacket. It wasn't a traditional tux by any means, but it suited Ren.

He was ready as he was ever going to be for this night. Somehow, it had turned into more than a dance, and not just because of what it meant to the town. It was important for Ren, too. His classmates embraced him for getting them this night. Now everything had to be perfect.

With a spring in his step, he left his bedroom out in the garage to join the rest of the family in the backyard. He'd been planning to skip dinner entirely, but Lulu wouldn't let him. He'd been too busy to eat any real food all day. He needed something in him if he was going to dance all night.

He approached the picnic table to the sound of cheers and the adorable catcalls of his young cousins. His aunt Lulu was very impressed. "Look at you! Oh, Ren, you look *fantastic*."

"Wow! You lookin' sharp, Ren!" Sarah cheered.

Amy danced on her chair. "I wanna go to the dance."

"Careful, Amy," Ren warned as he took her down off the chair. "You're still in Bomont. No dancing."

Ren caught his uncle giving him the once-over. "I see what you're doing," Wes said. "Two-color suit. That wouldn't work on me. People'd think I just wore the wrong pants."

Now Ren was concerned his choice may not have been right. "What? You don't think it works?"

"You make it work," Wes said with a proud nod. "Just like everything else. The car. The council. That bow tie."

"I like the bow tie," Amy said.

Ren had barely sat down before Lulu wrapped an enormous bib around his neck. The girls cackled with laughter. Even Wes was amused. Ren modeled the look for Sarah and Amy. "What do you think, girls? Should I wear this to the dance? The bib with the pink hippos?"

Wes laughed along with them now. "Well, no one else will be wearing it."

"I don't want anything getting on your clothes," Lulu said. "You look so nice. Don't let me forget to take your picture."

He'd be sure to remind her. No one had asked to take his picture in a while. He couldn't remember the last time he had a night he wanted to remember.

Wes held out his hands. "All right, Amy. Why don't you say grace?"

The family all held hands, but Ren interrupted before the little one could say anything. "Hey, uh, Amy? Sorry to interrupt, but I think I got one in me. You mind if I give it a go?"

Amy sighed with melodramatic relief. "It's about time."

Ren closed his eyes and searched for the right words. The thought had come up on him suddenly. He hadn't planned anything to say. Of course, he'd heard enough of their prayers around the table over the past few months to know the basics, but he had something more personal in mind.

"Dear God," he began. "Thank you for the food we are about to eat. I know that I haven't spoken to you in a long time. And the last time I did, well, I may have said some things that weren't so nice. But things are better now. I'm living with my family. I got two little partners in crime that help me every morning with my hair. But I help them with their braids, so we're even." Sarah and Amy giggled.

He paused to gather himself. The last thing he wanted to say wasn't easy to do out loud in front of his family, but he had to do it. He needed them to hear. "And, God, if you ever get around to seeing my mother, tell her she was right. I belong here. I belong in Bomont."

The silence around Ren told him he'd done it right. But that silence stretched on a bit longer than comfortable. He leaned over and whispered to Amy. "What do I say now?"

"Say 'amen,'" she replied.

"Amen."

* * * * *

She should've gone with the purple. Or the silver. Something flashier that hugged her body better. And the hair— why'd she put it up? She hardly ever wore it up. For a girl who was usually sure of every move she made, Ariel was having the hardest time getting ready for a simple dance.

Not that there was anything simple about this dance. It was probably the first and last of its kind—at least for her. She wouldn't be surprised if Andy Beamis rented out the storage room to the high school every year. Maybe even open up a hall for weddings and such. But this was the only time she ever imagined she'd be going to a dance before graduation. This one had to be special.

In the mirror, she saw movement over her shoulder. How long had Momma been standing in the doorway watching her? Probably long enough to think her daughter had lost her damn mind. "You look stunning," she said.

"Is it okay?" Ariel asked. "Is it too simple?"

"Darlin', simple and elegant is something to strive

for, not retreat from," Momma said. Ariel took a good look at herself. The pale pink dress really didn't look so bad. The spaghetti straps made it feel almost delicate and sexy at the same time. But the hair?

"Should my hair be up?" Ariel asked. "I've got it pinned up in the back."

"Up. Definitely up." Momma tamed a few stray hairs for her. "After a night of dancing, it's going to all come down anyway. But you can't really go to a prom without a corsage."

Ariel hadn't noticed the flower in her mother's hand until she held it up. Tears welled in both their eyes. The pink roses went perfectly with the dress. "It's beautiful. You didn't have to do this."

Her mother smiled. "I didn't."

Now the tears really threatened to flow. She couldn't let that happen; it would ruin her mascara. Ariel took a few deep breaths to calm herself, then went to see Daddy. He was in his office at the old electric typewriter that he sometimes used to type out his sermons. The look on his face when he saw his daughter threatened to bring her tears right back. He hadn't looked at her that way in a long, long time.

"No red boots?" he asked.

"Not tonight." She held up the corsage. "Could you help me pin it?"

Moore stood up. He took the corsage, but held on to her hand. "It's not that kind of corsage. It goes around your wrist." He slipped the band around her hand. "There."

This close, Ariel could smell her daddy's cologne. The scent always reminded her of Bobby. He used to sneak into Daddy's stash back when they were little and pour on way more than any one person his size would ever need. Daddy would yell at him for wasting the cologne, but always with a laugh in his voice.

"You don't understand how hard it is for me to let you go out that door," her father said. "I just want what every parent wants. I want my children to come home safe."

Ariel could see in his eyes just how much he was struggling. But she also recognized that he was beginning to understand that she could never come home safe if he didn't let her go in the first place.

"I know it's been hard for you," she said, with a catch in her voice. Her tears flowed freely now. "And I know I haven't made it any easier. I just don't want you to be disappointed in me anymore."

Her daddy took his handkerchief and carefully wiped the tears from her face. "Not at all. You're my angel. And I will always love you. *Always*."

He took his daughter into his arms. She breathed in his scent to keep it with her as they held tightly to one another, swaying gently.

"Hey, Daddy, guess what? We're dancing."

This brought a smile to his face. They swayed a bit

longer, enjoying their shared moment that had to end too soon.

"Okay," he said, reluctantly letting her go when he looked through the window and saw Ren's beat-up old car pulling up. "We can't keep your gentleman waiting."

She kissed him on the cheek. "Thank you, Daddy."

They walked out to the foyer together and Ariel said good-bye to both her parents. She was out the front door and closing it behind her even before Ren made it up the walk.

He was surprised by her sudden appearance. "I was going to come up and . . ." Then he really saw her, and stopped short. "Whoa."

"What?" She checked her dress to see if there was anything wrong. "What's the matter?"

"You're beautiful."

Oh. Ariel had been told that before. But this was the first time she ever really believed it. "Yeah?"

"Oh, yeah."

Ren took her arm and escorted her to the VW. It was a refreshing change from what she was used to. With a flourish, he bowed and went to open the passenger door for her.

It didn't budge.

"Is it locked?" Ariel asked.

Ren struggled with the handle. "No . . . it just sticks. I thought I fixed it."

He looked like he was going to hurt himself. "Ren, it's okay. I can go through your door."

He yanked harder. "No, I don't want you to."

Ren was so sweet, but it was starting to get really awkward. Luckily, Ariel saw a solution. "Okay, stop. Give me a hand." She held out her hand and nodded toward the open car window.

Ren picked up on the message. With a bright smile, he gently took her into his arms and lifted her feet through the window.

Ariel slid into the car effortlessly, taking care not to let her dress snag on anything. Once she was firmly in the seat, Ren ran around to the driver's side and hopped in behind the wheel.

They were on their way.

Chapter 24

Lit up as it was with white mason-jar lanterns around the entrance to the storage area, the Beamis Cotton Mill looked nothing like it did the day before. It was as if Ren and Ariel had been transported someplace else entirely when they pulled up in front of the building. Someplace magical.

Inside, the students of Bomont High seemed even more magical, transformed by elegant dresses and snazzy tuxedos, fancy as in any big city. A slow song played over the speakers: "Almost Paradise." It was almost perfect.

Except that not a single person was on the dance floor. They were all clustered in groups along the edges of the room, avoiding the center like it was a minefield. The only movement was the spinning disco ball overhead.

Ren feared the worst. Did the town council get to

them? Their parents? Was something wrong? "What's going on? Why isn't anyone dancing?"

"They're scared. I bet it's their first time ever at a dance." Ariel tugged at his hand. "C'mon. Let's show 'em how it's done. Dance with me."

Ren almost laughed. After all he'd gone through, he never imagined that anyone else in this town could simply be insecure about dancing. But tonight was so much more than a dance—it was an event. An event these kids had absolutely no experience with.

Ren escorted Ariel to the dance floor, stopping briefly on the way for a word with Woody. "By the looks of things," Ren said, "I'd say your offensive line doesn't have any backbone. Now move your team down the field, Captain."

Woody smiled. "Copy that." He turned to Etta, who was standing by the punch bowl, and formally bowed to his date. "If you'll excuse me, I gotta go crack some heads."

"By all means," Etta replied with a dainty wave.

Ren and Ariel stepped onto the dance floor alone, while Woody worked on getting them some company. He walked over to eight of his football players.

"Okay, huddle up." They did what their captain said, getting into a tight circle as though they were on the field. "Y'all see those women over there?" Woody pointed over at their dates, who had separated themselves from their guys the moment they'd gotten into the hall. The girls all pretended like they didn't know they were being discussed from across the room. "They're not looking for a first down or even a touchdown. They want some men to take charge and ask them to dance. Now, are you gonna sit on the bench, or y'all gonna man up?"

The huddle broke as the offensive line crossed the dance floor to their girlfriends. Woody held his hand out to Etta. "My lady?"

Etta accepted his hand. "My man."

Ren and Ariel shared a smile as more couples joined them on the dance floor. Once the football team was on the field, other people straggled out in twos and fours, slow dancing to the music.

· · · · ·

Outside the dance, Willard held out his hand to help Rusty out of his truck. She'd always been the kind of girl he could pal around with, but tonight was the first time she seemed like a woman to him. It had nothing to do with the dress or the makeup or the hair; it was actually more the change in Willard. He finally saw her through the right eyes.

He was kinda smokin' himself, in his Western-style tux with the black bolo tie and matching cowboy hat. "You know," Rusty said as she dropped down from the truck, "when you told me you were going to wear a cowboy hat, I didn't know how I would feel about it."

He stepped back so she could take in the full picture. "Well, now that you've seen me in it, what's the verdict?"

She moved closer to him. "I think you're sexier than socks on a rooster."

Willard was almost speechless, but he managed a reply. "That may be the nicest thing you ever said to me."

"Well, I mean it." She held onto him and added, "Stud."

The rumble of an engine ended their moment. A familiar truck pulled into the parking lot. Chuck was behind the wheel. His followers, Rich, Russell, and Travis, hopped out of the back as soon as he stopped. None of them were dressed for the dance.

"Remember, you promised," Rusty whispered to Willard under her breath. "No fighting."

"Hey, Willard," Chuck said as he got out of the truck. "You look pretty tonight."

Willard clenched his teeth and refused to lose his temper. "What can I do for you, Chuck?"

It was Russell who answered. "We got some business to take care of with our friend McCormack."

"C'mon, guys," Willard said, trying to contain his anger. "Cool it. No fights tonight."

Chuck stepped up to him. "I get it. No fights." His hand flew up to Willard's face, flicking the hat right off his head. "But we sure as hell didn't come here to dance."

Willard clenched his teeth to bite back the things he wanted to say. Insults wouldn't help. He picked up his hat off the ground and dusted off the dirt. "Well, fellas, that's what we came here to do, so you'll have to excuse us."

Willard took Rusty gently by the arm and started to guide her to the door, but Russell and Rich blocked their path. He took a deep breath and released Rusty's arm, not wanting to get her caught up in whatever was about to happen. He had no intention of fighting, but he couldn't say what Chuck and his buddies were going to do.

"You know what?" Willard said. "That doesn't mean y'all can't have a good time. Seems to me like you all got a foursome here on your own."

Chuck's sucker punch to the gut caught Willard off guard. The jackass laughed as Willard went down hard on his knees.

Rusty raced to his side, but Rich and Travis grabbed her. They pulled her away as Russell cracked him across the face.

"Stop it!" Rusty screamed as she struggled against them. "Let me go! Willard!"

Willard was on his knees. The world spun, but he had promised he wouldn't fight. "What do you want me to do?" he asked her. "They started this."

"Finish it!" she yelled. "Kill the sons of bitches!"

That was all Willard needed to hear. He slammed his fist between Russell's legs and launched himself at Chuck, pounding the loser into his truck.

Rusty put up a fight of her own, kicking and stomping

at the guys holding her. She bit Rich's arm. He screamed like a little girl.

* * * * *

The high-pitched screech broke through the silence in between songs. Something was wrong outside. Ren quickly and quietly went to check what was happening. Even though he told Ariel to stay behind, she was with him every step of the way. They both had no doubt what they'd find.

Their suspicions were confirmed as soon as they were through the door. Willard and Rusty were holding their own, but they were outnumbered.

Ren evened up the odds a bit, calling out to Chuck.

"What's up, Twinkle Toes?" Chuck said. "Come on over and get your ass kicked."

Ren ran right for him. "Yeah, you're a hero when it's four to one."

He collided with Chuck, taking them both to the ground, rolling in the gravel. Rich and Travis let go of Rusty so they could jump into the fight against Ren and Willard.

Chuck grabbed a crowbar and swung it at Ren, who dove out of the way, avoiding each blow from the metal with fancy footwork.

Willard beat Rich to the ground with his bare hands before slamming Travis into a nearby car, knocking the wind from him. Travis fell to the ground. He didn't get up.

"There you go!" Rusty cheered on her guy. "Kick his ass, Willard!"

The girls were distracted by the fight and didn't see Russell grab a loose brick. He was about to pound Ren from behind when a fist came out of nowhere. Andy Beamis knocked him out with a single punch.

"Play fair, you punk," Andy said as he stood over the groaning teen.

With Chuck's minions out of commission, the fight was finally even. Just Chuck against Ren. Or it would be, if it weren't for the crowbar.

Chuck threw the crowbar at Ren's head, then rushed him. Ren ducked the flying metal and met Chuck halfway with a powerful kick to the jaw.

Chuck dropped to his knees. He could barely keep his eyes open as he tried to focus on his opponent.

Ren grabbed the back of Chuck's head and lifted him to his feet. He pulled back his fist. "The race is over, Chuck. You want stars or a checkered flag?"

"Eat shit, you son of a—"

"Stars it is." Ren let his fist fly, clocking Chuck on the chin with a punch that sent him reeling backward. He landed on the ground with a spectacular thud.

Ariel and Rusty cheered, leaping into their boyfriends' arms and showering them with victory kisses, much better than anything they would get in the winner's circle.

Ren broke free of Ariel's embrace and extended a hand to Andy. "Thanks, Mr. Beamis."

Andy gave Ren a gentle shove toward the party. "How about a little less boxing and a little more boogie? It's like a morgue in there."

Ren took Ariel's hand in his. "I'm on it."

As Ren got to the door, his excitement took over, fueled by the adrenaline from the fight. He let go of Ariel and rushed onto the dance floor. "Hey, what's going on? I thought this was a party. LET'S DANCE!"

The DJ served up just the right song, and a familiar beat came through the speakers. The couples who had been swaying slowly broke apart so they could move. The ones who had abandoned the dance floor came back, stomping to the music. The dancing was wild and frenetic.

Willard confidently led Rusty onto the dance floor, put his dusty black hat on his head, and shot her a grin. "You might wanna back up, sweetheart. I don't know how big this is gonna get."

He busted a dance move that was part line dancing, part hip-hop bounce, and maybe a bit of little-girl enthusiasm, courtesy of Sarah and Amy. Rusty couldn't believe what she was seeing. "Shit-howdy!" she exclaimed.

Willard calmed himself down and grabbed Rusty, spinning her onto the dance floor. The room erupted into exactly what Ren said it would be, a joyous celebration of life.

Everyone was having a great time, moving to the music, dancing, and cracking each other up laughing at their crazy moves. And yeah, maybe there was a little lewd and lascivious mixed in, but only a touch.

Ren had one more surprise up his maroon sleeves. "Willard, you ready?"

"Let's do it!"

They each grabbed a bucket filled with colorful confetti and dumped it into the exhaust chute. Ren hit the switch that turned on the fans and sent the confetti shooting out over the dance floor. It rained down on the dancers like magic dust—the perfect way to top off an evening they'd never forget.

Everyone shouted and cheered. They started a line behind Ren as he danced his way down the length of the floor, slapping hands with Willard and Woody, saving a huge smile for Ariel when he reached her on the other side.

Ren was no longer a stranger in Bomont. He was an outsider no more.

The song that had started the tragic story ended it with joyous abandon. Everyone in the place knew the words and sang along.

Everybody cut—Footloose!